TWO BARE ARMS

A DEAD COLD MYSTERY

BLAKE BANNER

RIGHTHOUSE

ISBN-13: 978-1-63696-002-9

ISBN-10: 1-63696-002-2

Cover design by: Damonza

Printed in the United States of America

www.righthouse.com

www.instagram.com/righthousebooks

www.facebook.com/righthousebooks

twitter.com/righthousebooks

PRAISE FOR THE DEAD COLD SERIES

Here are some of the over 100,000 five star reviews left for the Dead Cold Mystery series.

"Rex Stout and Michael Connelly have spawned a protege."

AMAZON REVIEW

"So begins one damned fine read."

AMAZON REVIEW

"Mystery that's more brain than brawn."

AMAZON REVIEW

"I read so many of this genre...and ever so often I strike gold!"

AMAZON REVIEW

"This book is filled with action, intrigue, espionage, and everything else lovers of a good thriller want."

AMAZON REVIEW

DEAD COLD MYSTERY SERIES

ONE

It was autumn in New York. Or, to be more accurate, it had been autumn in New York. Now it was November, and lovers who blessed the dark did so in their apartments, where it was warmer and drier than Central Park. The leaves that had made picturesque, russet drifts just a week earlier were now turning to sludge, and the branches that had held them and released them gently onto the sidewalks now reached bare, skeletal, and cold toward heavy, gray skies.

I held Dehan's coffee in both hands, and the warmth made me shudder. Through the windshield, I saw her step out of her apartment block. A gust of damp wind caught her hair and whipped it across her face. She scowled and ran toward me as a few fat drops of rain splatted on the glass. It was that kind of day.

She climbed in and slammed the door, making cold, shuddering noises. I handed her her coffee, and as she hunched over it, I reached around to the back seat, grabbed a folder, and dropped it onto her lap. She sipped and eyed me.

"Want to tell me about it while I warm up?"

I pulled out into the traffic and sighed deeply.

"My parents never really understood me. I felt very isolated as a child, which made it hard to relate to people as an adult. I think that's why I broke up with my fifth wife . . ." She was staring at me with hooded eyes. I grinned. "Oh, you meant the case?"

"Funny. How can you be funny at eight in the morning in November?"

"And a Monday. Kind of guy I am. This is the case of the two arms found in a lockup in an alley between Revere Avenue and Calhoun Avenue."

"Throggs Neck. Barkley Avenue. Forty-Fifth Precinct is right there on the corner."

"That's the one."

"Gotcha. So, is that true?"

"That two arms were found there? Sure."

"No, that your parents didn't understand you and you were married five times."

"No, of course not. My parents thought I was the neighbors' youngest kid. They used to feed me because they thought I looked hungry and neglected. Pay attention, Dehan. There's a double row of self-storage units. It is eight units long, and each unit is about fifteen feet deep by ten feet wide. Monday, December 5, 2005, Peter Smith opens up his lockup and finds, lying on top of a stack of boxes, two female arms, severed, with some skill, through the shoulder joint."

She sipped, then asked, "Were the arms bare, or dressed?"

"Excellent question. The arms were not dressed. They were bare. In fact, the investigation ground to a halt after no more than a week because there was zero forensic evidence other than, obviously, her fingerprints and DNA. The only witness was Peter, and he had an alibi. He was with his wife. So, there was nowhere left to go with the case."

She blinked out the windshield for a while, hunched over her coffee, watching the wet, gray procession of people and vehicles. The only sounds were the listless squeak and thud of the wipers.

"No forensic evidence and no witnesses?"

"Nope."

"What's your plan? You know somebody who can read tea leaves?"

"Nyeah . . . no. I think we can do a little better than tea leaves. Sometimes, little grasshopper, people just ask the wrong questions."

"And you are going to ask the right questions."

"I hope so."

"We just passed the turnoff for the station house, so I guess we're going to Revere Avenue."

"Yup."

WE PULLED up outside Peter Smith's at eight thirty a.m. It was a large, Dutch-style red brick with a small front lawn and six steps up to a white front door. I rang the bell and waited. Nothing happened, and I glanced up and down the road. Across the way I saw a man open his front door and stand staring at me. He was in his mid to late thirties, medium build with dark hair. He called over, "Good morning! Pete and Jenny have taken the kids to school. They should be back in twenty minutes or half an hour."

His house was smaller, detached, with a white fence and gate. He stood watching us, smiling. We crossed the road, and I showed him my badge as we pushed through the gate.

"Detectives Stone and Dehan . . ."

"I kind of figured."

I frowned.

Dehan said, "Yeah? How's that?"

He pointed at us both with both his index fingers and spoke as though he were asking questions. "Your physical interactions? The way you relate to each other? You're obviously not a couple. You're kind of purposeful? On a mission? Most likely cops." He pointed at his front door. "You want to wait inside? It's awful cold."

I nodded. "Thanks. That'd be great."

He held out his hand. "Bob, Bob Luff."

We shook, and he led us inside.

It was an open-plan living room, dining room, kitchen with a big bow window that gave a clear view of the Smiths' house across the way. I glanced into the kitchen, saw two mugs and two plates by the sink. He was making his way to the kettle.

Dehan asked him, "Been here long, Bob?"

"About fifteen years. We moved in a year before Pete and Jenny. We're the vets! Coffee?"

I told him we'd just had some.

He made himself a mug. He was frowning. "Pete okay?"

I smiled. "Yeah. Just some routine questions about a cold case. If you were here twelve years ago, you may remember it."

His eyebrows rose. "Oh?" He pointed at the chairs and sofa. "Sit. My wife will be back soon," he added, as though that made it okay to sit. "Twelve years ago . . ."

Dehan said, "George Bush was president, Chris Brown was in the charts with 'Run It!,' *Harry Potter and the Goblet of Fire* was a hit at the box office, it was your third year in this house . . ."

He watched her say all this with a slack smile. She sat, and he sat too. I sat where I could see the Smiths' house. I added, "And Peter found two arms in his lockup."

He kind of jerked upright and sighed with closed eyes. "Oh, my goodness! That was twelve years ago." He glanced at Dehan. There was something reproving about his expression. "Somewhat more memorable than Chris Brown! I remember it well. Poor Jenny was distraught. As was Pete! Imagine! You open your lockup, garage, whatever, and there, staring at you, two arms! It doesn't bear thinking about. It's sort of . . . It always makes me think of Schrödinger's cat."

"Schrödinger's cat?"

He smiled at me. "Well, according to the Copenhagen interpretation, as illustrated by Schrödinger's cat, until the box is opened, the cat is both alive and dead."

I frowned.

He sighed. "The mystery was never solved, then?"

I pulled a face. "Sometimes we look so hard at the essential facts that we miss crucial evidence that is not immediately obvious. Thinking back to that time, Bob, does anything stand out in your memory? Anything that at the time struck you as unusual, remarkable . . ." I shrugged. "Even if it doesn't seem relevant. You never know how things are going to link up."

He sighed again and gazed out at the gray sky. The trees were bowing and tossing, and the odd fusillade of raindrops strafed the glass in the window.

"My wife will be more use to you than I. She has an elephantine memory. Remembers *everything*, in minute detail, and she *notices* things. What sticks out for me from that time is that Pete was away a lot. He was a rep for his company, and he'd spend one or two weeks away at a time. That was hard for Jenny." He suddenly looked scandalized at what we might have thought and waved both hands at us, like he was trying to rub out what he'd said. "Not that she . . . in any way at all! She was and is an exemplary wife!" He settled down. "It was just hard for her, you know?"

I could feel Dehan's irritation from where I was sitting. I smiled at her. She asked him, "Did you happen to notice any people in the area who seemed out of place, strange behavior . . . anything of that sort?"

He gave a small, humorless laugh. "Well, this *is* the Bronx, but within the usual bunch of crazies and weirdos, no, nothing stands out in my memory. Nothing that made me stop and think, 'Hello! What are *they* up to?'"

Across the road I saw a car pull up, and almost immediately afterward, a second car pulled into Bob's drive. I stood. "I think that's the Smiths, and your wife."

He stood, peering out. "Oh, yes indeed."

He hurried to the door and opened it to his wife. She was large and comfortable, the way a sofa would be large and comfortable if it could cook chocolate brownies. She looked at us in surprise while her husband explained our presence, and she seemed distressed that we were leaving.

"Do come again," she said, "if you think we can be of any help. I'll see what I can remember!"

Outside, across the street, Jenny was going through the door. Peter had stopped on the steps, with the listless drizzle speckling his face. He watched us approach, frowning. I guess he had also noticed our lack of physical interaction. We showed him our badges, and he said, "What's this about?"

Dehan answered, "It's about the arms you found in your lockup twelve years ago, Mr. Smith. Could we come inside and talk to you?"

I added, "We won't take up more than a couple of minutes of your time."

He seemed to snap out of his frown and said, "Of course! Of course! Come in . . ."

Jenny was standing in the hallway looking anxious. She was pretty, about thirty-six, well groomed, with intelligent blue eyes. She was saying, "What is it, honey?" addressing her husband but looking at us.

"Well, I don't know yet, sweetheart, do I? Let's find out." To us he said, "Will you have some coffee?"

We said we would, and he sent his wife to make coffee while he sat us down. "Has there been some development, Detective Stone?"

"We periodically review cold cases, Mr. Smith. Sometimes a fresh perspective, a new set of eyes, can make a difference. I know it was twelve years ago, and I know you went over it all with the detectives at the time, but I was hoping you could talk me through exactly what happened that weekend."

He spread his hands and kind of shrugged with his face, like he thought we were wasting his time and ours, but he had to be polite.

"I can spare you ten minutes, Detectives, but I have work to do."

Dehan smiled sweetly and said, "We appreciate any time you can spare us, Mr. Smith."

He sighed and seemed to gather his thoughts. Outside, the trees swayed, and a sudden squall threw a handful of rain at the window.

"I'd been away the week before. I got back on the Friday. I was pretty tired and spent the weekend relaxing, doing some shopping . . ." He smiled. It was almost reproachful, like we had somehow been responsible for what happened. He said, "The kind of thing you wouldn't normally remember twelve years later, unless you found a couple of severed arms in your lockup!"

From the kitchen, Jenny said, "Oh, Peter!"

He turned to stare at her with a rigid face, but he didn't say anything. She came and sat next to Dehan with a tray of coffee.

"It was horrible," she said. "We'd had such a nice weekend. It was lovely to have him back . . ."

She smiled at him. He didn't smile back.

"Do you want to take over, honey? You want to tell the story?" Her cheeks colored, and she handed Dehan a cup. As she handed me mine, he continued talking. "Sunday we did things in the house, started getting Christmas decorations out. I was going away again on the Wednesday, so we had to get everything ready for when I got back. Jenny can't do that kind of thing on her own."

I glanced at Dehan. I could see her jaw muscle pumping. Peter spread his hands.

"Nothing else happened Sunday. Monday morning, I went to the lockup to get a box of baubles and paper chains, lights, that kind of stuff. And there, on top of the boxes . . ." His eyes seemed to glaze, and he shook his head. "At first I thought they were part of a manikin, and I was wondering how the hell a manikin had got into my lockup. Then I looked closer and it dawned on me, they were real. I actually fell down."

He stared at me. I could imagine him in a counseling session, looking at his therapist in the same way.

"I ran. I vomited at the end of the alley. Poor Jenny had to come and clean it up."

She simpered at us.

He ignored her. "Naturally, I immediately called the police." He shrugged. "I'm sorry. That is really all I can tell you."

Dehan cleared her throat. She had a notebook on her knee, where she had been scribbling things. She was looking at it now. "You said you were away the week before . . . What work did you do at the time, and how long were you away?"

He seemed to grow, like he was about to tell us he was a special advisor to the White House.

"I represent the CAC Corporation—Canadian American Chemicals. Back then I was a representative, and I had to do a great deal of traveling . . ."

Dehan smiled. "You mean you were a sales rep? Were you traveling by car or by plane, Mr. Smith?"

His face hardened. "Is it relevant?"

"We don't know."

"I started out as a sales representative, that is correct. All my traveling was by car, and very exhausting it was too. I put in my hours and was rapidly promoted to area sales manager, and now I work mostly from home. Which reminds me . . ." He glanced at his watch.

Dehan was still smiling. "So how long were you away on that occasion?"

"I seem to recall it was a week."

"Where had you been?"

He thought for a moment, looking up at the ceiling. "Michigan."

"And you were off again the following Wednesday, to . . . ?"

"Ohio and Indiana. Now, if there is nothing else . . ."

I said, "Yes, there is. I would like to see the lockup."

"Now?"

"No. If it's not a problem, I would like to borrow a key and come back later to have a look at it. I don't need you to be there. If you have no objection, of course."

He looked put out but got up and went to find the key. He pulled it from a drawer and handed it to me. "I don't know what you hope to find there after twelve years, Detective."

"Neither do I, Mr. Smith. But you'll be the first to know when I find it."

The door closed behind us, and we stood on his porch. Dehan zipped up her jacket, and I looked across the road. The drizzle had turned to steady rain. Bob was watching us and raised a hand to wave. I didn't wave back. I hunched my shoulders and ran to the car.

We sat for a moment, listening to the hollow drumming on the roof.

"Impressions?"

"Why do women put up with guys like that?"

"That may or may not be relevant, little grasshopper."

She sighed. "I know." She gazed out at the rain making ever expanding rings in the puddles. I watched her with the dull light on her face. "I'd like to believe he got home, chopped somebody's arms off, stuck them in his lockup, and then called the cops. But I have to admit it's highly improbable. Plus, I *feel* he was telling the truth."

I turned the key in the ignition and pulled away into the road. "Feelings are notoriously unreliable. Even women's feelings. Whatever our mythology may say about your intuition, it is highly fallible. That may be exactly what he did. You want to know what I saw?"

She looked at me. "You didn't feel, you saw. You are such a guy."

"I saw him go rigid every time his wife spoke. I also saw her cowering every time he addressed her. And I saw that he only ever addressed her to put her down."

I turned into Lafayette. She was nodding, like I didn't "get" her. "See?" she said. "That, all that, is what I *felt*."

"Quit making excuses. You want to be a psychic, feel. You want to be a cop, *translate* those feelings into analysis. That means pictures and words."

"You are so harsh."

"Your Honor, I just kinda *felt* like he was a bad guy. Call it women's in-choo-ishun."

"Take a hike."

TWO

WE SPENT MOST OF THE DAY DOING BACKGROUND research. I wanted to know about the CAC Corporation and Peter's role in it over the last twelve years, and I had Dehan looking into who owned the other lockups in the alley.

At lunch I went to get some beef sandwiches from the deli, and we sat in the gray light from the window and chewed in silence for a bit.

"I went to see the new captain, John Newman," I said after a bit. She glanced at me but kept chewing. "Nice guy. I asked him what he wanted to do with the cold cases. If he wanted us to keep going or return to regular cases."

"What did he say?"

I made a smile that was rueful. "He said we made such an awesome success of the Nelson case, he wants us to keep going for now." She rolled her eyes but didn't look too upset. After a bit I added, "I told him, you know, I'm a dinosaur, but you, you're young, you're smart, you want to be building a career." She gave me the dead eye and bit into her sandwich. "But he said it would look good on your CV and he'd review it in six months."

She said, "What? I'm no good as a partner? You want to get rid of me?"

"Don't be stupid, Dehan. I'm looking out for you."

"Like my dad?"

"No . . . Well, kind of, but no. Like your partner. You could thank me."

"Thanks. But don't. I want a transfer, I'll ask for one."

We returned to our research. I glanced at her. She seemed to be smiling. I said, "Gets dark about six. We'll head over to view the lockup at a quarter to."

"You want to view it in the dark?"

"Yup."

"Don't tell me why. I can figure it out."

"Good."

It had stopped raining by six, but the air was cold, and the occasional icy drip brushed your face or made small ripples in the puddles. We left the car on Barkley Avenue and entered the alleyway on foot. It formed a dogleg to the left, where one tall lamppost cast a dispirited, yellow light on the blacktop. It was quiet, and our footsteps echoed loud in the dark stillness.

We came around the corner, and I stopped. On either side of the alley there were redbrick walls to a height of maybe eight feet. Fairly dense evergreens topped the walls most of the way along. There were eight units on either side, with roll-down metal doors. The lighting here was not much better. Three lamps were bolted to the facades and cast a dead, yellow light that made the shadows seem deeper.

I retraced my steps and took a look back at the road. It was brightly lit and busy. I said to Dehan, "How busy do you figure it is on the weekend?"

She walked back to join me. "Saturday, busy. Sunday it's probably pretty quiet, especially at night."

I nodded. "So, I'm trying to figure out what happened here. What have I done? I've brought the arms in the trunk of my car. I've parked down there on Barkley Avenue, what, fifty yards from the cop shop? I've taken the arms out of my trunk, or from the back seat of my car, and I have brought them into this alley."

Dehan was staring, like she could see the car parked down there by the road. "Have you got them in a big garbage bag? Or in a duffel bag? Or are they just bare?"

I nodded, chewing my lip. "Right. And what has made me choose this alley, so close to the station house?"

"It's dark. It's lonely. Maybe you've driven past a few times and spotted it. Either way, for some reason, you know it."

"Okay. So I park my car. I grab the arms, and I bring them up here. I get to this bend, and I see, if I didn't know already, that there are sixteen units. All locked. What would you do?"

Unconsciously, she curled her arms like she was holding a heavy bundle. She stared down the alley. The far end, maybe a hundred yards away, was in deep shadow. "It depends what my objective is. If I just want to get rid of them, I'd take them to the end and dump them in the shadows."

"Right, and for now we are assuming that that is what this guy wants to do. So let's stay with that idea for the moment. Instead of doing the obvious thing . . ." I stopped and sighed, and topped it off with a shake of my head. "Dehan, when you use a public toilet, if you walk in and find all the cubicles unoccupied, which one do you automatically choose?"

"The one at the far end by the wall."

"More than eighty percent of people do that, because somehow it feels more private."

"But this guy chooses a cubicle just past the middle, in the full glow of a lamp."

We walked up to the unit. I bent down and unlocked the padlock. I went on, "I dump the arms on the ground, and I take the time to pick the lock. I push up the roller blind . . ." I stood and heaved the blind up. It made a loud, clattering noise. "And either I risk switching the light on, or I have a flashlight." I turned and pointed at her. "If I have the arms in a bag, I take the trouble to remove them and place them on a pile of boxes, just here."

I indicated a spot halfway down on the left.

Dehan said, "If it's a plastic refuse sack, maybe you're worried about fingerprints. In fact, most bags will have some place where you might find a print."

"So, he's not panicking. He is acting deliberately. I think the whole pattern of behavior involved—from coming to this particular alley, selecting and opening this particular unit, and placing the arms on the boxes—tells us that the whole thing was deliberate and not opportunistic."

She nodded. "Yeah."

"So that leads us irresistibly to a conclusion . . ."

"Either Peter put the arms here himself, or somebody chose to put them in Peter's very lockup, for a particular reason. Maybe a warning, an attempt to frame him . . ."

I scratched my chin. "So far I haven't found a single thing in Peter Smith's past that suggests he has any enemies, or is in any way involved in gambling or crime."

"So if somebody isn't trying to frame or incriminate him, why choose his lockup?"

"What is it about his lockup that would make somebody with two severed arms choose to leave them here?" I stepped out into the damp darkness. The pools of yellow light made the shadows black. I looked at the silent, dead roller blinds. "Take me through who owns them, Carmen."

"That whole side opposite was bought up about fifteen years ago by GCS, a local export company that specializes in IT products. This one here on the left of Peter's belongs to a supermarket on the avenue, but twelve years ago it belonged to Hank Junkers. At the time, he was a member of the Hells Angels, and he used it to store his spare parts, tools, yadda yadda. He lived not far from here with his girlfriend, Lynda Holly. He has a history of violence and assault, some against women. Three on that side belong to a large pharmacy and a whole-food shop. And the three on this side belong to a bar and the local newspaper. An initial survey of employees doesn't throw up any flags."

"You like the Hells Angel."

"He kind of sticks out." She walked away from me and stood in the glow of one of the lamps. It made her into a desolate silhouette and cast a twisted shadow at her feet. She was staring back down the alley, the way we'd come. Her voice sounded strange, too loud. "They have a row. Maybe he's drunk, high, or both. He knocks her about and kills her. Now what the hell is he going to do with her? So he cuts her up into manageable portions and distributes her around town. He's not going to put her in his own lockup. So he puts her in the one next door." She shrugged. "Picking locks is the kind of skill he might have."

"December 2005, January 2006, there were no dismembered bodies found in the New York area. What did he do with the rest of her?"

"He's got a few big rivers to choose from."

"Where they will never be found. Especially if he loads her down with a few engine parts."

"Exactly."

"So what made him put the arms in Peter's lockup, instead of dumping them with the rest of her? If he put her legs in the river, why not her arms?" I stuffed my hands in my pockets and took a couple of steps toward her. I couldn't see her eyes. "No, whoever put those arms there made a deliberate choice about the location. That leads to one irresistible conclusion. He was not hiding them —he wanted them to be found. He would do that for only one of two reasons. To throw a scare into Peter, which suggests a threat or a criminal connection, or because he knew that Peter would be going into his lockup within days rather than weeks."

"He *wanted* them to be found . . . ?"

"It's the only thing that makes sense. So we have to ask ourselves, what makes a killer hide a whole body so well that it is never found, but put the arms in a place where it is guaranteed that they will be found within a day or two?"

She stood staring at me with invisible eyes. The rain started to patter again, not heavy but enough to make you wet. After a moment she returned to the black mouth of the unit. I joined her and saw her shudder.

"I can't think of a single reason you would do that, unless you were trying to intimidate somebody. And we have already established that was not the case. So . . . ?"

"So you're thinking like Carmen Dehan. If you ever killed somebody, it would be for a practical purpose, and you'd either call the cops as soon as you'd done it, or you'd make damn sure the body was never found. But one thing is for sure. Unless it was a real bad case of revenge, you would not enjoy it. You would never feel the desire to boast about it."

The rain started coming down harder, hammering on the steel roof and hissing in the trees.

"A murder for pleasure? Placing the arms as a tease?" She turned to look at me, and now her eyes were luminous in the darkness. "You're talking about a serial killer. You think that's what this was?"

I stared a long time at the puddles without answering. Was it? I watched their ever expanding and interlocking ripples and the complex interference patterns they made with each other. Above them the trees bowed and danced and whispered wet whispers, and the cold air crept in around our feet and clenched damp fingers around my ankles. Then, just as suddenly as it had started, the rain eased and paused, and I said, "Come on. There's an Italian restaurant up the road. It'll be warm, dry, and quiet. Let's have a pizza and a couple of beers."

THREE

The bell chimed as we stepped in and stamped the rain from our boots, stripping off our coats. The place was empty except for a waiter who was walking toward us, beaming. An open fire was burning over on the left, and as the waiter approached, I smiled at him and said, "We'd like a table by the fire."

His face lit up, and he spread his hands like I'd said the very thing he'd been waiting all year to hear. "*Ma certo! Certo che puoi!*"

He led us to a table for two, held Dehan's chair for her, and looked inquiringly at me. I asked him for two beers, and he took our coats away to a coatrack near the door. Then he went to get the beers. Dehan was staring at the fire, and I could see the light from the flames playing in her eyes.

"Don't get me wrong, Stone. I follow your logic, and I see where you're coming from. But it just seems a hell of a conclusion from very little evidence." She paused. "Some might say no evidence at all."

"Is that a feeling or a thought?"

"Come on. Give me a break. You're basing a theory that the arms belong to the victim of a serial killer on what? The fact that they were found in a lockup?"

The waiter arrived with two frothing beers, and I asked him for two sirloin steaks with plenty of french fries, easy on the salad. I glanced at Dehan. "That okay with you?"

"I thought we were having pizza."

"In this weather? You've got to be kidding." I nodded at him. He bowed and went away. "Okay, Dehan, go wild here, really go out on a limb, push the boundaries of credibility and find me one single theory that is more credible than mine."

She was silent a long while, staring at the coals. Eventually, she sighed. "You always wind up with the same problem—why didn't he do the same to the arms as he did to the rest of the body?"

I sipped my beer. "And the related question, which to me is more important: Having successfully disposed of the whole body, what benefit does he get from leaving the arms somewhere where he knows for sure they will be found?"

"What benefit does he get . . . ?" she muttered.

"The benefit is right there, in the question . . ."

"That they will be found."

"Precisely. Which leads us to the next question. In what way is that a benefit to him?"

She sighed again. "And we're back to square one. He is either throwing a scare into somebody, or . . ."

"Or the benefit is subjective. It gives him a kick, a thrill, an ego boost. And that leaves us very firmly in one place. Serial killer territory. Somebody who kills for pleasure."

"If you're right, Stone, the problem becomes much more complicated. This woman could be from anywhere in the United States, and the rest of her could be scattered from here to California."

"Yup." I nodded. "And the lack of motive means we have no idea what kind of man we're looking for."

"Serial killers are always men, right?"

"Male. There was one case of a woman serial killer, but she was emotionally and intellectually male. The overwhelming majority are men. Within that, there is no profile for a serial killer.

They tend to have average to below-average intelligence, though a few are highly intelligent. They tend to be underachievers and feel inadequate, though some have risen very high in their professions as doctors or soldiers. They tend to be victims of violent, unhappy families, though again, one or two have come from perfectly normal, middle-class families. The only thing they really have in common is that they invert the normal progression for killing."

The waiter, wearing an air of triumph, delivered our steaks, gave a little bow, and withdrew.

I cut into mine and watched the blood ooze onto the plate. It was perfect. Dehan said, "What does that mean?"

I chewed, enjoying the rich flavor, watching the luminous beads of rain slide down the black glass on the window.

"Normally, in a murder, there is a very clear progression. The killer and the victim meet and form a relationship. Often it's a loving relationship, sometimes a business relationship. Always it's a close relationship. The relationship provides the motive for killing—jealousy, vengeance, financial gain . . . Those are the big three. And from the motive springs the desire to kill. So relation-ship leads to motive leads to desire. The serial killer inverts that process."

She sat back and sipped. "So the serial killer first forms the desire to kill. He doesn't care who. He just wants to kill. From the desire he develops the motive—the desire *is* his motive. And then he develops a relationship with his chosen victim."

I nodded. "Exactly. The relationship may be short, a few minutes or hours, or it may be longer. But usually he will start by stalking, then sometimes he will progress to kidnapping . . ."

She waved her knife at me. "I have read that they fall into roughly two categories: organized and disorganized . . ."

I shook my head and spoke with my mouth full.

"Three. Organized, disorganized, and mixed. If I'm right, and it is still a big if, we are most likely to be dealing with an organized serial killer."

"Why?"

I gazed down into the flames in the fire. "Organized serial killers plan their killings methodically. The placing of the arms in the lockup, the absence of any forensic evidence, the absence of any witnesses—it all suggests methodical planning." She nodded and continued eating. I carried on talking, thinking aloud. "Often they will abduct their victims, kill them in one place, and then dispose of the body somewhere else. As you said, if I am right, she could have been killed anywhere in the U.S.A.

"They often target prostitutes. Not only are hookers likely to go voluntarily with a stranger, they are also *less* likely to be reported missing. He will have control over the crime scene and have a good knowledge of forensic science. He will also follow reports on the news relating to his crime, because he will feel a kind of narcissistic pride in what he's done, as though it were some kind of achievement.

"Organized killers often seem normal. They have friends, romantic relationships, and even get married and have kids. They tend to think they are a lot smarter than they are. Their IQs tend to be around ninety to ninety-nine."

I could tell by her face that she'd been thinking while I was talking. Without looking at me, she asked, "They often keep trophies, right?"

"Yup."

"Could the arms have been a trophy?"

"I know where you're going. It's possible, but they're a bit big. But then you face the same question. If the killer intended to keep them as a trophy, why put them in Peter's lockup? If Peter was the killer, which is what I think you are driving at, why report them?"

She had finished her steak, and she sat back, narrowing her eyes at me. My steak was getting cold, so I started eating while she watched me.

"I have no grounds for this at all, Stone. But I am just imagining Jenny going to get the decorations from the locker without telling Peter. I can see her falling down, then running home hysterical, and Peter taking charge, like the pompous little prick he is . . . 'Just let me handle everything, little lady . . .'"

She was right. It was a compelling image. I spoke through a mouthful of french fries. "He had the job for it."

"So we need to be looking at other states for dismembered bodies."

I drained my beer. "Yes, we do. We must also avoid fixating on Peter. I am also interested in Hank the Hells Angel and his girl-friend, Lynda. And we should explore the other tenants—the export company, the whole-food shop, and the chemist."

She tipped her empty glass around a bit while I ate. The warmth from the fire was soporific. After a moment, she waved her glass at the waiter and winked at me.

"You can't have one. I can." When he had delivered it and gone away, she said, "I thought that too. The arms could be Lynda's. She didn't have a record, so when they ran the prints and the DNA, they wouldn't have got a hit."

"Tomorrow morning, bright and early, I'll find out where Hank is living these days while you check for dismembered female bodies in late 2005, early 2006. Talk to Bernie at the bureau. Also, on the off chance, talk to the sheriffs and PDs in Michigan, Ohio, and Indiana."

"What about girls who went missing at that time?"

"We will probably have to go down that route eventually, but without fingerprints or DNA, and nothing to compare dental records with . . ."

We talked a little longer, and when she'd finished her beer, I looked at my watch. She raised her hand like she was hailing a cab and said, "This one's on me, Sensei."

I smiled. "I know better than to argue. Next one's on me."

"You bet."

Outside, the road was deserted. The puddles looked black and oily, and they rippled with small gusts of cold wind and drizzle.

The light from the streetlamps and the shop fronts lay orange and listless across the water, like it had lost all hope of ever being bright and merry. We climbed in the Jag and slammed the doors. I fired her up, and Dehan gave an almighty yawn.

"Let's go home, pardner."

FOUR

IT WAS ANOTHER DULL, DRIZZLING MORNING WITH occasional rolls of thunder, like some giant moving big furniture across the clouds. Dehan spent the morning digging up what she could about the IT company, the chemist, and the bar, and I tracked down Hank. He had spent some time in California and Arizona, but now he was back in New York with his own workshop, Hank's Bikes, fixing and customizing hogs in Brooklyn, on Surf Avenue, right by the Brooklyn Cyclones.

We grabbed a couple of sandwiches and ate them in the car as we drove down through Queens, just ahead of the lunch-hour traffic. Brighton Beach in November is not the most depressing place on Earth, but that's about the best that can be said for it. It's gaudy and brassy and desolate, and seems to be populated by people who have swapped hope for various forms of psychosis.

Hank's Bikes was a big prefab situated on a huge parking lot just off Surf Avenue. I parked outside, and a tall, blond, bearded guy in his midthirties came out wiping his hands on a cloth. He wasn't looking at me or Dehan; his eyes were fixed on the Jag.

"Sweet ride, mister. Real thing, huh. Right-hand drive—what is she, '65?"

"1964, 210 brake horsepower."

"You got the original plates?"

"Framed at home."

"You lookin' to sell her?"

I laughed. "No way, not no how."

He smiled. "Shame. She's worth a bit, especially with the original plates. Spoke wheels. Man. She is sweet."

Out over the Atlantic, thunder boomed and then rolled. I said, "Are you Hank Junkers?"

He nodded. "You're askin' like that, you gotta be cops."

I showed him my badge, as did Carmen.

"Detectives Stone and Dehan. We're just following up an old case, and we'd like to ask you some questions."

He jerked his head toward the workshop and led the way in. As he walked he said, "I ain't seen Zak for over ten years. And I ain't been in trouble since I came back from Tucson. That's gotta be five or six years ago."

The light inside was dull, but he had a couple of arc lamps set up where he was working on a Harley. I had a look. It was good, precision work. He was fastidious and detailed. A perfectionist.

"What's this about?"

"You used to have a lockup in the Bronx, at the back of Revere Avenue."

He shrugged. "So?"

"What can you tell me about the people who had the next unit?"

He looked at me like I was crazy. "That was ten, twelve years ago! I don't remember." He thought a moment. "What side?"

"On the right of yours."

He stared out at the wet, gray lot. It had started to rain again, and cold air was fingering its way in. "Yeah. That was Pete." He laughed. "He was a young guy, 'bout my age, but man, was he stuck-up. He didn't approve of me. Used to lecture me on how I would never make anything of my life if I didn't plan for the future. He had a cute wife. Jane . . . ?"

Dehan smiled. It was a troubling, conspiratorial smile. "You and Jenny ever get it together?"

He snapped his finger and leaned his ass on his workbench. "Jenny! Nah, I tried once, but she didn't want to know. I'm talking like we were old buddies, but he was always away and she was always in the house. I only saw them a few times in a couple of years." He screwed up his face. "Why you askin' me about Pete?"

I ignored his question. "What about Lynda?"

His face went hard. "What about Lynda?"

"You ever see her these days?"

He shook his head. "You wanna know about Lynda, you better ask Zak. I ain't spoken to Lynda in twelve years. Since I was in the Bronx . . ." He paused, putting two and two together. "What's this about? Do I need a lawyer?"

I shook my head. "Nope."

Dehan said, "Who's Zak?"

"Zak was the son of a bitch who took Lynda from me. We was in the same chapter."

"Of the Angels?" she asked.

He nodded. "We were like brothers. More than brothers. And he knew that I was crazy about Lynda. But . . ." He paused, thinking. "For the 2005 Christmas rally, we all gathered at Camp Kaufmann, outside Holmes, near Poughkeepsie. Man, he would not stop comin' on to her. Givin' me all this shit about how we were bros, and bros should share everything . . ."

Dehan asked him, "How did she take it? Did it make her mad?"

He made a face that looked genuinely sad. "Nah, she was laughing, going along with it. Telling me not to be so uptight."

"What happened?" I said.

"We got into a fight. I told her to choose. It was either me or him. She chose him."

Dehan said, "Fight? What kind of fight?"

He sighed. "Look, back in the bad old days, I hit a few

women. I regret that more than I can say and more than you'd probably believe anyway. But I done my time for it, and I am reformed. But right then she was with Zak and two hundred other brothers, so if I'd tried to lay a hand on her they would have gutted me and thrown me in the pond. I was mad enough to give her a hiding, the way she treated me that night. But I didn't." Suddenly he looked mad. "You gonna tell me what the fuck this is about or not? I ain't answering no more questions till you do."

I sighed. "What date was that rally, Hank?"

"I just told you I ain't answering no more of your questions till you tell me what this is about."

"Twelve years ago, two arms were found in Peter Smith's lockup. We are trying to find out who they belong to, and who put them there."

He gaped at me. Then he gaped at Dehan for a bit and then gaped at me again. "Two *arms*? Like arms and legs? Two *arms*? And, what? You think *I* put them there? You think they're Lynda's arms and I put them there? Why the fuck would I do something as dumb as that?"

"I don't know, and I am not saying you did." I asked again, "What date was that rally, Hank?"

He blew out, making an exaggerated noise, and spread his hands. "How the fuck should I know? It was the first weekend of December, Friday through Monday."

Dehan checked her phone. "Second to the fifth. What day was your fight with Zak and Lynda?"

"The last day. Man, I can't believe you are trying to pin this on me. I fuckin' walked away. You can ask Zak. Ask any of the fuckin' bros. I walked away."

"Where can I find Zak?"

He was silent for a while. "He's got a club up in Maine, 'bout thirty miles west of Portland, on Sebago Lake. It's called the Hell-fire Club." He looked at us fixedly, first Dehan and then me. "If you tell him I said where to find him, he will kill me. You'll have my blood on your hands."

"Don't worry, Hank. We're not out to get anybody hurt." I pointed at the bike. "It's nice work. Keep it up."

He didn't answer. He just watched us hunch through the rain to the Jag and climb in. As I fired up the engine, I glanced across Dehan. Hank was standing in the doorway with his arms crossed, looking like a Viking in blue overalls.

The wipers set up their squeak/thud rhythm, and we eased our way out onto Surf Avenue again. Dehan looked around at the long, straight rows of dreariness and shook her head. "When I die, if I've been really, really bad, I'll be sent somewhere like this." I laughed and she glanced at me. "At least in hellfire, you can scream and shout because you're in pain. You're feeling something, right? But this! To eternally feel nothing but boredom . . ."

I grunted. "To feel nothing is more painful than to feel pain. You're deep, Dehan."

"So what did you think of him?"

"I thought he was a nice guy. I liked him."

She leaned her head back and closed her eyes. "You're something, Stone. One of a kind."

"What? You didn't like him?"

"Like him? I'd like to whip his ass all the way back to Poughkeepsie."

"You think the arms are the arms of his lover?"

"It's at least possible."

"Let's see what Zak says tomorrow."

FIVE

DEHAN MADE CONTACT WITH SOMEBODY AT THE Global Computer Shipping Company, so she went to talk to them and I drove out to Maine to see if I could find Zak and the Hellfire Club.

I took the I-95 all the way to Portland, following the coast, then Brighton Road and the Roosevelt Trail out to Raymond, on the lake. It took me a little over five hours, and it rained all the way. For my money, New England is probably the most beautiful place on Earth. In spring and fall, there is no probably about it. But in winter, there's something sinister about the heavy, lowering clouds and the trees, like cold, naked hands reaching up with crooked fingers into an unforgiving sky.

It was two in the afternoon as I left Portland behind me and started west through dense woodlands of tall, dark pines that seemed to go on forever. At twenty past, I was skirting the lake outside Raymond, looking for Cape Road. The water was flat and gray, like a mirror reflecting the heavy clouds overhead. I finally found it just outside South Casco and turned left, winding through five or six miles of thick forest. After about fifteen minutes, I finally came to a fork in the road. The left fork was narrow and overgrown, and plunged down, like a track through dense jungle. A wooden sign with an arrow on it read *This Way to the Hellfire Club.*

The track led to a driveway, which in turn snaked through pines and came out at a broad grass clearing with an old, gabled house in the middle. It was big, three stories with a basement. At a glance, I figured there must be seven to ten bedrooms, if they had converted the loft.

I followed the drive to the front of the house. There were half a dozen choppers, an old Land Rover, and an early-model '90s Jeep sitting there. I parked where it would be awkward for them to leave, just in case, climbed out, and slammed the door. As I headed toward the porch, a man stepped out the front door and stood looking down at me. He was tall, six two or three, lean, and rangy, but you could tell he was hard and tough too. He was wearing jeans and cowboy boots and a black T-shirt, and he had a forked beard that reached down to his belt buckle, which was shaped like a skull. He was anything but original, but he was the real thing.

I said, "Are you Zak?"

"You come into my domain, you don't get to ask me who I am. I ask you who you might be."

I pulled out my badge and showed it to him. "Detective Stone of the NYPD."

"You're off your turf, NYPD. Why don't you get back in your pretty, foreign car and get the fuck off my land?"

I sighed. Originality was clearly something I was not going to find at the Hellfire Club. "Because if I do, then I'll have to come back with a warrant, the FBI, and guns. And all I want to do is to ask you a few questions about an investigation that probably has nothing to do with you in the first place. I'm getting wet out here. Why don't you invite me in, give me a cup of java, and I'll be gone in fifteen minutes?"

He smiled a smile that he probably intended to be cruel, but I was too wet to care. He said, "Sure, why not?" turned, and walked back into the house. I climbed the stairs after him. Over the door there was an elaborate carving of two devils holding a scroll on which was written *Lasciate ogne speranza, voi ch'intrate*. Abandon all hope, ye who enter here. Nice.

He was standing in the shadows inside the house. As I stepped over the threshold, he pulled a cigarette from a pack and lit it with an old brass Zippo. The walls were covered with erotic murals. Some were psychedelic, evocative of the '60s. Others were impressionistic. Some were even good.

There was a huge face of Crowley done in red and black, like the famous picture of Che. Written underneath it in flowing, gold script was *Do as thou wilt shall be the whole of the law.*

Zak dropped into an old leather sofa and pointed to a chair. I sat, wiping water from my face and my hair. Zak gave a shrill whistle, and a girl of maybe twenty, with hollow eyes and a stud in her lip, came in in bare feet. She looked sad. Zak pointed at me and said, "Bring the cop a towel." She hurried away at a little run. He smiled at me. "She's an acolyte."

She came running back a couple of minutes later with a big, fluffy towel and handed it to me with a small bow. I took the towel and said, "Don't ever bow to me. Have some self-respect. Don't ever bow to anybody, unless they're bowing back."

Zak said, "Go." She left. "What do you want to ask me, Detective Stone?"

"I want to know about your big Christmas get-together in 2005, in Connecticut, near Holmes. You remember that?"

His face was empty. He just smoked and stared at me. Eventually he said, "What's to remember? That was twelve years ago. We spent four days stoned, high, and drunk."

"I'm trying to trace two people whom I believe were at that rally. I think you had close ties to them."

"All bros have close ties, man."

"One was your best friend. The other was your girlfriend."

He laughed. "Girlfriend? What, were we dating? Or just fucking and getting stoned together?"

I listened to the rain for a bit while he finished wheezing his laugh. When he was done, he said, "I don't know what to tell you, man. I fucked a lot of chicks. I can't remember all the ones I fucked in 2005."

"Her name was Lynda."

He shrugged.

"How about your best friend? Or don't you have them either? Do you just fuck them too?"

It was a curious thing to watch. His expression stayed the same, but the smile drained out of it, turning it into an ugly, dangerous mask. His voice was quiet.

"I don't fuck guys, Detective Stone. Sometimes I fuck them up, bad, but I don't just plain fuck them. What was this guy's name?"

"Hank. You remember Hank?"

"Yeah. I remember Hank."

"Do you know where I can find him?"

"No. I ain't seen Hank since that rally in 2005."

"How about Lynda?"

Any trace of a smile had left his face. "I already told you, I don't remember any Lynda."

"You remember Hank, but you don't remember Lynda. I find that kind of hard to believe."

"I think you had better leave now, Detective Stone. It's going to be getting dark soon, and these roads can be real dangerous at night."

I sat forward. Somewhere in the house, the wind made a door creak. A squall of rain lashed the window. "You see, Zak, I know that you remember Lynda. So I have to ask myself, what is it that's making you pretend that you don't? What makes you want to hide your relationship to Lynda from the cops so bad that you would actually threaten that cop's life? And it is that kind of question that is going to have me and a dozen Feds swarming all over your house like flies on shit. I wonder what we're going to find? Besides the coke and the meth, do you think we'll find any body parts?"

He held up both hands and shouted, "Woah! Take it easy, Mr. NYPD. There ain't nobody threatening nobody here. And there ain't no fucking bodies buried in my garden. Take it easy. Chill."

"Chill? Next time you threaten me with violence, Zak, you better be prepared to make good on your threat, because I am going to whip your sorry ass all the way back to New York, where I will throw you into Rikers and watch you rot there for the rest of your miserable life. And believe me, there will be no law of Thelema there."

"Okay—it was just talk. Take it easy."

"Tell me about Hank and Lynda."

He flopped back his head and closed his eyes like I was boring him. "Hank was a bro. He had a chick, and she was cute, hot, you know?" He looked at me, like he was actually asking me if I knew what a hot chick was. "But Hank was soft. He *cared*. You can't care in life. It doesn't work that way. He was always talking about bros, and loyalty, and being there for each other . . ." He laughed again. "Man . . . and he was all dewy-eyed and going to pieces over this bitch. So I tried to help him."

"Help him? How?"

"I told him, let's fuck the bitch together. Lose your respect for her, man. Treat her like the piece of trash she is. You let a woman get inside you and you are *fucked*. I mean, you do not fuck them, they fuck you and they fuck you bad. I have seen many a bro go down because he went soft over a chick."

"So did he agree?"

"No, man. He got mad. Which proves what I am telling you. Women are evil. They are like poison. They are there to serve us and bring us to manhood, nothing more. You start treating them with respect, they fucking eat you alive. Like the man said, if you're going to women, don't forget the whip."

"Spare me your philosophy, Zak. What happened?"

"Nothing. I tried to make him see sense. She was fucking all over me. He gave her a choice, him or me. She made the wrong fucking choice. She chose me. That's women, man. Fucking stupid. He left. I never heard from him again. Somebody told me he went out west."

"What about Lynda?"

"I fucked her, used her for a day or two, and told her to get lost. It was what she deserved. It was a shame about Hank. He was stupid, but he was a bro. He couldn't see I was trying to help him."

"Yeah. You're a stand-up guy."

He surprised me by giggling.

"Where did she go?"

"The party broke up on the fourth day. She probably got a ride with somebody. I don't know, man."

I looked at the murals on the wall, stared at Crowley's big, bald head with his bulging eyes. "You're a devotee of Crowley, huh?"

He smiled. "He's the man."

"You practice his rituals?"

He watched me for a bit before answering. "Some."

It was growing dark outside. The rain had settled into a steady downpour. I stood. "He died in poverty, in a boardinghouse in Brighton, you know."

"Yeah, and his followers are some of the richest, most powerful men in the world."

There was a heavy footfall on the stairs. A large man with long hair and a long beard stepped into the room. It was hard to make out his features in the dusk. He stared at me for a long moment, then turned to Zak. "They're ready."

Zak smiled at me. "We're having a ritual, Detective Stone. We found a virgin, and we're going to cut out her heart and eat it while it's still quivering with life. You want to stay and join in?"

"Maybe next time."

"Drive careful, Stone."

I stepped back out into the wet dusk and ran to my car. I climbed in and slammed the door. I had a pack of tissues in the glove compartment and used a couple to dry my hair and my face.

I switched on the wipers and looked through the windshield at the house. The windows on the third floor were glowing with a flickering, limpid orange light. Candles.

I looked at my watch. Four p.m. I fired up the engine and headed back toward New York. I felt tired, but I knew it would be at least ten before I got home.

Do as thou wilt shall be the whole of the law.

I thought about that as I crawled through the narrow lanes toward Raymond. The orange cones of my headlights made a moving tunnel in the blackness. It was Rabelais, not Crowley, and it was inscribed over the great gate of Theleme. More things crept into my memory.

Sir Francis Dashwood, in the eighteenth century, established several Hellfire Clubs in London and Dublin. Their motto was "Do as thou wilt shall be the whole of the law," borrowed from Rabelais. Ben Franklin had been an occasional visitor to those clubs. The patrons were eminent and powerful.

Then, a hundred years later, Aleister Crowley established the Abbey of Thelema in Cefalù, on the north coast of Sicily, and adopted the motto used by Dashwood for his clubs. He called it the law of Thelema.

Ritual magic. Ritual murder. It was certainly the province of the serial killer. I tried to visualize Zak murdering and dismembering a woman. It wasn't difficult. Did those arms, then, belong to Lynda?

SIX

In the end I got home at one, had a hot shower, and fell into bed. I'd been driving for over twelve hours, and every part of me ached. I ached in places I didn't even know I had.

I had dark dreams about dark houses with black doorways that led to even blacker places, down ever darker, narrower passages. I surfaced slowly as it dawned on me that the doorbell was buzzing, dragging me out of sleep. I didn't know if I was grateful or not. It was still dark, I still ached, and I was still tired. I looked at my watch. It was seven. I groaned and leaned out the window.

Dehan was standing in front of my door doing a weird bouncing thing.

"Why are you bouncing?"

She looked up at me. A cold wind was blowing her hair across her face. "Because it's cold and wet. Let me in. Why are you still in your pajamas?"

I pulled my keys out of my pants on the chair and threw them down to her. "Make some coffee and don't ask dumbass questions."

I showered cold, hot, cold, then dressed and went downstairs. She'd made a big pot of coffee and also pancakes and bacon.

"If my mother were here, she'd tell me to marry you."

"If my dad were here, he'd tell me to stay clear of you. 'Don't make the same mistake I made. Marry a nice Jewish boy.'"

I sat down and she poured coffee and put bacon on my plate.

"You told me your parents were crazy about each other."

"They were. He loved annoying her, and she loved being annoyed by him. She'd end up throwing her Havaianas at him, and they'd crack up laughing."

"Cute."

"It was. How'd you get on?"

"This means you're itching to tell me how *you* got on."

"You first."

I ran through my conversation with Zak. About halfway through, she stopped eating and just stared at me. By the time I came to the whole Aleister Crowley, Abbey of Thelema bit, she was neglecting her coffee. I told her what I saw when I left and said, "He definitely ticks some of the boxes."

She drizzled maple syrup on a pancake. "So he's mad at Lynda. He thinks it's her fault his best pal walked out on him. He takes her away somewhere. They do some kind of crazy, satanic ritual. He kills her and takes the arms to what he *thinks* is Hank's lockup. The arms are a crazy symbol of sorts. Brothers-in-arms. Arms of friendship. Whatever. But he makes a mistake and puts them in the wrong lockup. Not a serial killer, but a crazy."

"Something like that is a distinct possibility. What about you?"

She grabbed her hair and tied it in a big knot behind her neck. It was a very feminine action that was strangely at odds with the image she usually cultivated.

"I met Dave—David Hansen. He's the overall sales manager of Global Computer Shipping. Twelve years ago, he was what I guess you'd call a shipping clerk. The company operates mainly online selling refurbished computers, hardware, and software. You buy it online from their website, they ship it to you."

"That's why they need the lockups—to store the computers."

She nodded. Thunder rolled in the distance. There was a steady slapping sound from water spilling from a gutter in the garden.

"The guy has an eidetic memory. He remembered the case. He was there that Monday, collecting some computers. He remembered the cops asking him a few questions, but he had nothing to tell them except that he owned the units opposite."

"So . . . ?"

"So I remembered some details of the general profile you described, of the organized killer. Dave told me he followed the case in the papers and on the news for the next few days and was disappointed when it just fizzled out and no arrests were made. I asked him if he knew who the lockup belonged to. He said he had met him briefly and sold him some computers. The guy has a *real* problem with interpersonal skills, especially with women. Zero eye contact, speaks real quiet, like he's talking through clenched teeth, and I get the impression he is pretty OCD. His office and his desk were not just neat. Everything was regimented and organized according to shape, size, and color."

"It's not much to go on."

"I'm not done. I asked him where he was that weekend, the third and fourth. He said he was away at an IT conference in Los Angeles. He's a computer nerd and attends conferences on a regular basis. He lives with his mother. There's more . . ."

"Okay."

"I decided to do a background check to see if he had any priors."

"He has?"

"He's been arrested on three occasions for downloading child pornography. On each occasion he denied it and was released because they couldn't find the material on any of his computers."

I slumped back in my chair. "Nero Wolfe had too many clients, and we have too many suspects. Though child pornography does not of itself suggest he's a serial killer."

She shook her head. "I know that. But it is a coincidence that he displays a number of the characteristics often displayed by serial killers, and his company owns the units opposite Peter's."

"Yes."

I stood and started clearing the plates while she tipped her mug this way and that, watching the cold coffee stay on a level plane from every angle. I started washing.

"We have Peter. Evidence against him, such as it is, is that he displays misogynistic behavior toward his wife, he owns the lockup where the arms were found, and twelve years ago he had a job that would have enabled him to commit murders in several states. Not a lot, really."

She stood, grabbed a tea towel, and started drying what I had washed. "Hank had a girlfriend who might fit the description of the owner of the arms. He had the unit next to Peter's and has a rap sheet including violence against women. His girlfriend may have gone missing at the time the arms showed up."

I handed her a wet plate. "We need to get on to that. We need to find where Lynda is. That is a job for today." I continued where she had left off. "Zak. Crazy as a box of frogs knitting wool bikinis. A disciple of Aleister Crowley, a Hells Angel, so no stranger to violence, a self-declared misogynist with a possible serious grudge against Lynda."

I noticed absently that she had put everything away in the right place. As she closed the cupboard where she had placed the plate, she rounded off, "Dave, nerd supreme, OCD, lives with his mother, his company owns all the units opposite Peter's, he is and was at the time of the murder frequently away at IT conferences. He turned up on the morning the arms were found, followed the case with interest, and was, quote, 'disappointed that it fizzled out.'"

"We need to check on that conference."

"I did. It was real, but there was no way to check if he was there."

We stared at each other for a long moment, holding each

other's eye. It was something we had got into the habit of doing. Finally, she said, "So what now, boss man?"

"Our number one priority right now is to establish whether the arms belong to Lynda, whether Lynda is dead or alive. So I want you on that right away."

"What are you going to do?"

"I'm going to check missing persons for twelve years ago, plus a year either side, girls in their early twenties, pretty, blond. I'm also going to check for reports of dismembered bodies, coast to coast."

As it was, I didn't get very far. We got to the precinct at eight thirty, and at ten fifteen Dehan put down the phone and said, "I found her parents."

"Already?"

"Holly isn't a very common name. I used the phone book, just the way you taught me, Sensei." She stood, slipping her arms into her jacket. "And you know what? That paper . . ." She inhaled noisily through her nose, closing her eyes and smiling. "Mmm . . . the smell was just *intoxicating!*" I sat watching her, wanting to laugh. She said, "You coming, or you just going to sit there and smirk all day?"

SEVEN

IT WAS A TEN-MINUTE DRIVE THROUGH THE HISS AND spray of the I-278 and then Bruckner Boulevard. And at ten thirty-five, we pulled up in front of a modern red brick on Throgmorton Avenue. It was pretty and leafy—or would have been if there had been any leaves on the trees. I killed the engine, then we climbed out and crossed the wet blacktop to climb the steps to the front door.

Dehan rang the bell and stood looking at me with flushed cheeks from the cold wind. Her hands were plunged in her pockets, and she was bouncing on her toes.

"I love this weather," she said. I shook my head, and she said, "No, seriously. It's honest, real."

"The weather is honest and real?"

She nodded and the door opened. There was a woman in an apron and carpet slippers. She had permed silver hair and a face that said she was broken but coping. We showed her our badges and told her who we were, and she ushered us toward her living room, telling us to come in out of the cold.

She sat us down at a dining table that she had set for tea and went into the kitchen, calling, "Robert! The detectives are here!"

She came in with a kettle and poured scalding water into a

teapot, while soft feet came down the stairs. A man with a bracket of soft hair around the back of his head and a sage-green V-neck sweater came in. He was smiling and had reading glasses hung around his neck. He held out his hand, and we rose to shake.

"Sit down, sit down. Marion has made an event out of this. She is hoping you will finally put us out of our misery one way or another."

Marion returned from the kitchen, and we all sat again.

I smiled at Marion and said, "I'm afraid not. But we *may*"—I stressed the word—"have found a lead that will help us to find out what happened to your daughter. We are reviewing a number of cold cases, and it seems your daughter's disappearance may have some connection."

Marion was holding the teapot halfway to Dehan's cup. Her expression was eloquent. It said that unendurable anxiety can become endurable when it becomes your everyday experience. She gave a small sigh and poured the tea.

"Is she dead, Detective Stone?"

Honest and real, like the weather. "We don't know, Mrs. Holly. That is what we need to find out. Right now, I'd like to know what Lynda was like as a person, about her relationship with Hank, and about the days leading up to the bike rally that weekend in Connecticut."

Robert drummed his fingers on the tabletop, and you could tell he was biting back tears. Dehan, in one of those surprising moments of tenderness she displayed sometimes, put her hand on Marion's shoulder and said, "I know this hurts, Marion. Don't give up hope. We are here to help you."

Marion clung to her hand, and tears welled in her eyes. I turned to Robert. There was nobody there to hold his hand. I am not given to moments of tenderness, but I was moved to lean forward and put my hand on his shoulder. He nodded and we sat in silence for a moment, listening to the interminable rain pattering on the patio, as though we were honoring the dead.

Marion sighed. "Where do I begin? She was a sweet, adorable

child. Full of spirit, mischievous, but with a great, kind heart. Then she hit fifteen and, like a lot of kids, she went a bit wild. She started going to parties, coming home late, drinking. I think she smoked pot a few times. We tried talking to her, but she just didn't want to hear what we were telling her."

Robert cleared his throat. "We made an appointment with a child psychologist. She told us we were crazy and we should go. She said she was fine and just having a bit of fun. We did go . . ." He glanced at his wife. "The psychologist told us we should maybe give her a bit more space, not become her enemy but go along with her a bit, then reel her in gently. She said a lot of kids went through this rebellious phase, then settled. We tried that."

"How did that work?" It was Dehan.

Marion made an uncertain face. "I think it was working. She introduced us to Hank, which was something. Robert didn't like him to begin with, but they started working out their differences, didn't you?"

Robert nodded, then gave a small laugh. "Hank liked to appear the tough guy, but it was more an act than anything else. What he really wanted in life was a family." He looked at me. "He was an orphan, you know? Grew up on the mean streets. I know something about that. He put on a big display to protect himself, but when we opened our arms to him, he began to soften, stopped showing off, was nicer to Lynda. Confessed to me in private that he was thinking of leaving his gang and asking Lynda to marry him. May God forgive me, I advised him to wait."

Marion shook her head. "No, Robert, you were right. She would have run a mile. As it was, the nicer he became, the more she started getting bored! A marriage proposal right then would have had her running for the hills!"

Dehan was giving me that "well, whadd'ya know?" look. I gave her my "I can't help always being right" look. I asked Marion, "Do you think she was bored enough of Hank to go off with somebody else from the gang?"

It was Robert who answered. "Yes. To be honest, I do. But she would have come back home first."

Dehan frowned. "How can you be so sure?"

"Because she had just got her bike license, and we were going out that week to get her her first bike, a Yamaha 250. She was out of her mind with excitement. She wanted that bike more than anything in the world."

Dehan narrowed her eyes. "I hate to be brutal, but these are Hells Angels. They're all about bikes. Is it possible somebody made her a better offer?"

Robert surprised me by smiling. "That's not brutal, Detective. It's a smart question. But the answer is, it was the bike she had chosen, partly because she loved it and partly because her friends in the club had advised her on it. She really wanted that bike. Only reason she wouldn't come back for it is if she couldn't."

Honest and real. The rain had stopped, but an icy wind was bowing the evergreens in the back garden. The bare trees, the skeletons with nothing left to lose, they withstood the wind better.

I asked him, "Have you got a photo of Lynda?"

Marion got up and went to a dresser. She came back with an album. Dehan chose a picture and snapped it on her phone, then WhatsApped it to me. She was average height, fair-haired, pretty, cute, and, by the way she was laughing, bubbly and fun. If you looked a little closer, she also had "trouble" tattooed in invisible ink over every part of her laughing self.

"One last thing," I said, still looking at the photo on my phone. "Would you, by any remote chance, have Lynda's fingerprints? Or a sample of her DNA anywhere?" I looked at them, and I could see the dread in their faces. I shook my head and smiled. "It is purely a routine question."

They both shook their heads in silence. They knew I was lying.

. . .

OUTSIDE, Dehan rested her ass on the hood of my car. The wind was dragging her hair across her face again, so she tied it in a knot behind her head and squinted at me.

"Hank is just a nice guy with a small character flaw where he beats up girls?"

I knew we weren't moving till we sorted this out, so I said, "Humanity is made up of seven and a half billion unique individuals, Dehan. And however much I may want to say what you want to hear, that won't change the fact that you cannot classify human beings according to type. You should know that better than anybody."

I opened the car and got in, slamming the door behind me. Knowing what I meant by that would be a physical need for her, so she would have to get in to find out. Then at least we could drive and argue. She walked around the car and got in, frowning at me.

"What exactly do you mean by that?"

I fired up the car and moved off.

"Come on!" I said, as though she was being slow. "You are a mass of contradictions! Everything you do, say, and feel is contradicted by something else you do, say, or feel. You are like Newton's third law."

She wanted to get mad but wasn't sure what Newton's third law was. "Is that the one about every action . . . ?"

"For every action there is an equal and opposite reaction."

She was silent, nonplussed for a while. "I don't know if I'm supposed to be offended or not."

"Of course not, Dehan. I would never say anything intended to offend you. I am just pointing out that you yourself are a profoundly contradictory person. If you can be full of contradictions, why not Hank? Maybe think less about what people *should* be, and more about what they actually *are*."

She was silent for about five minutes, so I tossed her my phone and said, "Give Hank a call. Ask him to come in." She looked a question at me, and I said, "There is a damn good chance he killed Lynda, don't you think?"

She made the call, and he said he'd be there early afternoon.

EIGHT

WE HAD TIME FOR A QUICK BITE OF LUNCH, AND HANK arrived at two. He looked worried. We showed him into an interrogation room and sat him down. As we sat opposite, he asked, "What's going on?"

Dehan surprised me by taking the lead.

"Just a few details that need clearing up, Hank."

"What kind of details?"

She was pensive a moment, looking at the tabletop. "Well, for example, the fact that you were considering asking Lynda to marry you."

He shrugged and frowned at us in turn. "So what? It was twelve years ago, and her dad advised me not to. He was probably right. She was so crazy right then, she would have dumped me on the spot. Who told you that, anyhow?"

I got in before Dehan could answer. "The thing is, Hank, it seems you were pretty close. Closer than you really gave us to understand. It was quite a surprise to me to discover that you were pretty tight with her dad. Her parents liked you."

He nodded. "Yeah. They were cool. She didn't deserve them." He suddenly screwed up his face. He looked frustrated. "What's your point? I liked her. I was pretty serious about her. She had nice folks. So what?"

"Okay, Hank, let me level with you. You tell me a story about how you are a badass Hells Angel, you got your bitch, you go to a rally and your bro comes on to your bitch, you fight like real guys. She ditches you and you ride off into the sunset. Plenty more bitches out there. Then I look into it and I find the substance of the story is true, but there are a few details that you left out. See, you are not such a badass, you don't really think of her as your bitch, and your bro— well, you were actually thinking of *leaving* the Angels because you felt you had finally found that family you never had as a kid. Now, I have got to be honest . . ." I sat back in my chair and looked at Dehan. "My partner thinks you're a scumbag who beats up on women. I don't. The more I learn about you, the more I see you as a basically stand-up guy who was badly lost but had the balls to find his way."

He gave me a look that told me I could stick my opinion of him where the sun don't shine. "Gee, thanks, Officer Stone."

I ignored him. Dehan stepped in. "Thing is, Hank, even if you are the stand-up guy my partner thinks you are, this new, gentler image of you has exactly the opposite effect from what it should have. Because it gives you one hell of a motive for killing her."

His face and neck flushed red. He half stood and his chair fell back. "I have just about had enough!"

Dehan was on her feet. "Sit down!"

"I left Lynda at that goddamn rally with that motherfucking asshole, Zak!"

I got to my feet. He watched me walk behind him and pick up the chair. I said quietly, "Sit down, Hank."

He sat. I sat and Dehan sat.

"Zak tells me he was only trying to help you realize that you can't trust women," I said.

"That's bullshit."

"You didn't tell me he was into Crowley."

He heaved a huge sigh and made a helpless gesture with his

hands. "I don't know. I figured you'd find out. You know? You're coming at me from every fucking angle. You think Lynda is dead? When you came to my shop, you said I cut off her fucking arms and put them in Pete's fucking lockup. Now you're saying you think I killed her. What the fuck, man?"

He had tears in his eyes. I felt bad for him, but I ignored my feelings. "How much were you involved in the whole ritual magic thing?"

"Not." He said it emphatically. "I got into the Angels for the bikes, and because it was the closest I ever had to a family. Zak was crazy about the whole Crowley thing. A lot of the bros were. They used to snort and have crazy rituals. They used to talk a lot of shit about going beyond the limits." He gave a humorless laugh and shrugged. He glanced at Dehan. "Sorry, but a chick has three holes you can fuck. So how far past the limits are you gonna go? You gonna fuck her in the ear? Sorry, I got no time for that shit. Snort. Fuck. You don't need to prance around in stupid robes and invoke the fuckin' Devil."

Dehan asked him, "Is that all they did?"

"I don't know." He stared down at his hands between his legs. He looked unhappy. "It seems like yesterday sometimes. Lynda was a sweet kid. I really liked her. She was just a bit wild, but she didn't mean no harm. I know what that is. Maybe I should have just picked her up and carried her away. I think of her involved in all that stuff and it kills me."

"You didn't answer my question."

He looked her in the eye. "I don't know because I never went to one of his stupid rituals. But I heard they sacrificed chickens and drank their blood. I never believed it, but maybe it was true. Those guys were crazy enough to do it."

I watched him a moment. "Could they have progressed to people?"

He blinked a few times. They were odd, soft blinks. A tear spilled from his eye, and when he spoke he sounded like he had a cold. "I sure hope not."

"Were you aware of any girls going missing during that time?"

He wiped his nose and his eyes on the back of his sleeve. "I don't know, Detective. I'm sorry. Most of the time we were drunk or stoned. Chicks came and went. All I can say is I wasn't aware of that, but it is possible. If you're asking me were Zak and his coven crazy enough to make a human sacrifice, I have to say yes. I think they were crazy enough. They did a lot of coke"— he made a gesture with his hand like he was showing me something on the table—"*because* they said it helped them to go beyond the limits. So if they went on a snort-fest and got into a crazy ritual, yeah. They could."

"What day did you leave the rally?"

"It was Sunday, late afternoon, early evening."

Dehan said, "The Sabbath."

"Where did you go?" I asked.

"I went home. Called a friend in L.A., told him I needed to get away from things."

"An Angel?" Dehan asked.

He shook his head. "Told me to go over. So I did. Ended up staying awhile, then went to Arizona, worked with a mechanic there for a bit, till I got her out of my system. Then came back and set up my business."

"By bike, obviously." He looked at me and frowned. "You left the rally, went home, and then to L.A., by bike."

"Yeah, of course." He stared at me awhile, then at Dehan. "Do you even know she's dead?"

I shook my head.

"This is all because of those damned arms?"

I nodded.

He pulled a face. "You're on the wrong track. If Zak killed her, and I can't see why he would, but if he did, he wouldn't cut her arms off and put them in a fuckin' lockup. Zak was all about sex and humiliation. All he ever wanted to do was get the biggest fuckin' hard-on drugs could give him, and fuck and humiliate everybody around him. And he believed that Satan gave him the power to do that. Cutting off people's arms . . ." He shook his head. "That wouldn't do it for Zak."

He put his hands on the table and stared at them for a moment.

"When I left, when I walked out of that tent and got on my bike, she was hugging him, holding him tight with both arms. He had his arm around her, holding a beer. And they were both laughing, like they thought I was having a jealous hissy fit and I'd be back in the morning."

"What were your last words to them, Hank?"

He looked at me like the question surprised him. "I told her she was a fucking bitch and she didn't deserve the family she had. And I told him he was no bro of mine, I never wanted to see his lying fuckin' face again, and I would never forgive either of them for what they done to me." He was quiet for a moment, remembering, then added, "Some of the bros around the fire were laughing, but most of them was pretty serious."

"How serious is that, when a woman comes between two bros?"

"It's pretty serious."

We were quiet for a few moments. I glanced at Dehan. She said, "I'm done."

I said, "Thanks, Hank. You've been helpful. We'll be in touch . . ." I left the words hanging.

He stood and left without saying anything.

I drummed the table with my fingers and absently studied Dehan's face, waiting for her to speak.

Eventually, she said, "It's just stories. There is no way of checking if any of this is true. How do we know he left on his bike? How do we know he didn't take a truck with a couple of bikes loaded on it? How do we know he didn't leave with Lynda?"

"His story fits with Zak's."

She looked at me. "You like Zak?"

"If Lynda is dead, there is a better chance Zak killed her than

Hank. I think we can be sure she stayed with Zak Sunday to Monday. I reckon Zak's jealousy over Hank was greater than Hank's jealousy over Lynda. Hank lost a girlfriend. Zak lost a potential disciple. He is a narcissist and a woman hater. I'm going to ask the Feds to send over a profiler and discuss Zak, Lynda, and the arms. We could be looking at two completely separate crimes here."

"We could, but it would be one hell of a coincidence, wouldn't it."

WE SPENT the afternoon wading through reports from all over the U.S.A. between 2003 and 2006 involving missing girls who fit what we imagined was the killer's victim profile, plus cases of dismembered bodies. It made for grim reading, but nothing raised a red flag. I phoned Bernie at the bureau and asked him to arrange for a profiler to come see us.

By six, I was beat and told Dehan I was going home. She said, "My car is at your place. I'll come with you."

We drove in silence through the darkness. Artificial light, mainly amber with washes of red and green, leaned in through the windshield and painted her face with lurid colors. The rain had stopped, but occasional spits gathered on the glass like broken, liquid gems. The wipers gave a desultory squeak and a thud, and then rested again.

It seemed like a long drive through the November night, but eventually I parked behind her car, killed the engine, and pulled the handbrake. She didn't move for a bit, then gave me a sad smile. I gently punched her shoulder.

"Shakes you up, a case like this, huh?" She nodded, watching me, waiting. I smiled. "You want to order in? I'll teach you how to play backgammon."

"You don't have to feel sorry for me, Detective Stone."

"I don't. I think of you more as an unwitting victim."

She sighed to cover her smile. "Okaaay, Stone, if it will make you feel better, I'll keep you company for a while. We can order in if you don't feel like cooking."

I climbed the stairs with her just behind me and unlocked the door. I pushed in and switched on the light. There was a note on my mat, with my name printed on it, *Detective John Stone*. I bent and picked it up. Dehan was at my shoulder. I opened it. It said:

"Well, it took you long enough . . ."

NINE

I SLIPPED IT INTO AN EVIDENCE BAG AND SEALED IT. Then I put it in my pocket and pulled my piece. Dehan stepped in with her weapon drawn, and I closed and locked the door. If the writer of the note was still here, they weren't leaving. I pointed to Dehan to cover the stairs, and I checked the kitchen. It was clear.

I went on to the stairs, and Dehan covered me from behind. We made the landing. There were four dark doors confronting us. I signed to Dehan to cover three of them and moved into the fourth. It was the small guest room. There was nobody there.

Dehan moved up to cover two of the remaining three, and I burst into the second spare room. It was a double and bigger, with two single beds. I checked between them and under them, and in the closets. It was clear.

The bathroom was clear too, and that only left my bedroom and the en suite bathroom. I burst in with Dehan behind me. The room was still and silent. Everything was as I had left it that morning. Except that I knew I had turned the bathroom light off, and now I could see light reflected on the closet door.

I looked at Dehan. I could see in her eyes that she had seen it too. She covered me again, and I stepped in. There was nobody there or in the shower. But there was another message.

He had mixed what looked like blood with soap in the soap dish and used it to write on my mirror.

YOU'D HAVE DONE BETTER TO LEAVE ME SLEEPING.

THE CRIME SCENE team turned up within twenty minutes and did a thorough sweep of the house. It didn't take them long. By half past nine, they had established that he had picked the lock, which I logged as one of his skills, he had gone directly upstairs, written on my mirror, come down, left the note carefully on the mat, and left. Careful observation had shown traces of a muddy shoe print under where the note had been. It was not my shoe or Dehan's, and there was no trace of shoe prints anywhere else in the house, ergo he'd slipped plastic covers over his wet shoes and left the note when he left.

Frank, the team leader, paused at the door as they were leaving. "We'll get a good DNA sample from the blood. The only question you have then is, is it his blood? You going to be okay? You want me to send a car from the precinct?"

I shook my head. "No. I don't want to scare him off. Let him grow confident."

"Your call."

He went down the stairs. There was a volley of car doors in the wet night, and they pulled away. I watched their red taillights disappear and turned to Dehan, who was standing behind me with her arms crossed, shivering slightly.

"You want me to drive you home?"

She shook her head. "You going to kick me out without feeding me? What kind of man are you? After all I've done for you."

I closed the door. "I need more than takeout."

I went to the kitchen and found a bottle of Turnbull Cabernet Sauvignon, 2013. I'd heard it was exceptional, so I opened it and poured two glasses. She watched me do it and said, "You're supposed to let it breathe."

I raised my glass to her, and she chinked hers against mine.

"Let us be grateful, Carmen, that *we* are still breathing. It can breathe while we drink."

She laughed suddenly. It was startling. "You're a riot, Stone. You're cool. Let me see what you've got." She opened my fridge and started rummaging in my cupboards. "Let's have spaghetti. You like spaghetti? I'll make spaghetti."

She made spaghetti and we finished the bottle. It was better after it had breathed.

Dehan had the spare room. I put the dead bolt on the back door and wedged a chair under the front door. I more or less slept, but if I slept seven hours, I woke up seven times imagining I'd heard something. It was probably wind and rain. But seven times I got up to check, and to look in on Dehan to make sure she was okay.

As soon as I saw the sky turning gray, I was able to fall asleep properly. But I caught an hour and a half at most, because at half eight, Dehan was cooking bacon and making coffee again. I groaned and dragged myself to the shower, then to the breakfast table.

As I sat, she put a plate of fried eggs, bacon, and toast in front of me, with a large cup of black coffee.

"Lots of protein this morning, Sensei. How many times did you get up last night? I counted seven."

"Seven."

"The bureau called."

I frowned at her.

"Your phone was on the table. It rang. The screen said Bernie. I answered. It was the bureau."

"What did they want?"

"They're sending over Dr. Fenninger at eleven to talk to us and review what we have."

"Good. Thanks, Dehan."

She sat opposite me and smiled. "God. I feel like your mother."

Special Agent Anja Fenninger was neat, petite, and aggressively efficient in a way that only neat, petite women can be. She arrived bang on eleven with blond hair and a luminous smile and said that she believed that if you were *in* time you would always be *on* time. Or it may have been the other way around. Either way, she was both. I looked for signs of rain on her neat blue jacket and her blond hair. There weren't any, and there was no mud on her shoes either. Neat, petite people can do that, effortlessly.

We found a conference room and sat around the table.

"What makes you think you're dealing with a serial killer?"

I outlined the investigation so far and highlighted the point about the arms. "It's hard to get around. If the killer was trying to dispose of the body and get rid of the evidence of the killing, then *A*, why didn't he do with the arms what he had successfully done with the rest of the body? And *B*, what prompted him to leave the arms in a place where he must be sure they would be found before long? Add to this the fact that that particular unit seems to have been chosen over the others, and it looks as though we may be dealing with an organized serial killer."

Agent Fenninger listened very carefully, not looking at me but gazing abstractedly at the table. When I'd finished, she blinked once and said, "I agree. Couple of things I want to clarify first, though. Profiling, in any field, is descriptive and not prescriptive. That is so much more so in the case of serial killers, because we know so little about them. Some psychologists suggest that there is actually no such condition as a serial killer. However, what we can do, and we do it rather well, is describe what we have seen and what seems to be typical so far." She gave a small laugh, as though somebody had just suggested something stupid. "That does not mean that serial killers are somehow required to follow the rules that we at the bureau have laid down."

I nodded. "Understood."

"Having said that . . ." She leaned back in her chair and said nothing while she stared at the ceiling. I stole a glance to see what she was staring at. All I could see were the shadows of the raindrops on the windows. "Having said that," she said again, "I am having trouble reconciling your suspect Zak with the arms. Zak is by definition chaotic and opportunistic. He actually sees himself as a wolf, roaming through a forest, waiting to see what life will bring him." She smiled, like she was about to indulge in some harmless flippancy. "You know the song from *Easy Rider*, 'Born to Be Wild'? Well, Zak is looking for adventure and, crucially for me, whatever comes his way."

Dehan sighed. We glanced at each other, and her face told me that what Agent Fenninger was saying made perfect sense to her. Fenninger went on.

"So, either we fit the careful placing of the arms in the lockup into an opportunistic, chaotic behavior pattern, or we dismiss Zak as a prime suspect." She looked up at the ceiling again, and I realized she had her list of suspects pinned up there. "Hank, if you have him as a suspect, would simply not fall into the category of a serial killer. Serial killers do not kill their partners. Almost, I would say, by definition." She sat blinking at the table a moment and added, almost impatiently, "I would say that is true of Zak as well, to some extent. In both Hank's and Zak's case, you are looking at killing driven by a motive. Which would put them outside the definition of serial killer."

Dehan interrupted, "That doesn't mean we discard them as suspects. It just means they have a motive, right?" She glanced at me. I nodded. Fenninger went on as though she hadn't spoken.

"Peter, who owns the lockup, could certainly fit into the profile of an organized serial killer. Clearly he has issues with women and seeks to humiliate and control them. Such a need for control often speaks to a profound, volcanic rage against women that cannot be suppressed. Women who are perceived as flirty, promiscuous, careless, thoughtless—who step outside of what the man considers appropriate or acceptable behavior—can trigger a profound, destructive rage.

"We also see a pleasure in taking control in a cold, methodical way. This feeds his ego and would be very much present in the aftermath of the killing. If you look into his past, you are typically going to find a mother who humiliated him, perhaps in public, and a cruel father, or perhaps no father at all. Either way, the father has abandoned him and left him to cope with the humiliation of his mother on his own, so that the only outlet for his rage becomes physical violence. But not against her! He dare not! It must be against an unknown woman, a blank canvas if you will, against which he can project the nightmare image of his mother that he has created in his mind and which he must destroy. So! Your question: Does Peter fit the profile? Prima facie, yes, but I would urge you to look into his childhood. You know . . ." She laughed suddenly. "He may be just a harmless prick!"

We smiled and she went on. "Dave, certainly, from what you have outlined, would fit the profile. He seems to have a tendency toward obsessive-compulsive behavior. Again, he displays a need to control his environment. His inability to relate may be due to a physical condition like severe dyspraxia or autism, but that inability to relate is a common feature of the organized serial killer. When it is, it is generally the result of a loveless and often violent home life as a child. The obsession with pornography, especially child pornography, is also a common feature. As before, it speaks to a need to control the love object, a fear that if he loses control of her, something bad will happen. She will hurt him in some way. He will lose her love.

"So, love is organized and controlled in a way where there is no risk of humiliation or rejection. You can see," she said, as though it were obvious, "how this can lead to narcissism, where love is directed toward himself, instead of toward the object of love. In the end, where masturbation is the only source of loving consolation, he *becomes* the object of love, controlling his environment and the women in it. I say women, but of course they are not real women, simply two-dimensional images."

Dehan said, "So any woman who upsets that two-dimensional relationship . . ."

"Could trigger very violent rage indeed."

Dehan stared down at the table, chewing her lip. Special Agent Fenninger leaned back and stared up at the ceiling again, consulting her list, and I stared out at November. It had started to rain again. The naked trees looked like bony hands that had been trying to claw their way out of their graves but had changed their minds because the weather was so awful.

Fenninger was talking again. "Now, the note and the message on your mirror. These tell me a couple of things. First, and most important for you, he is close to you. He knows you have reopened the investigation. Second, it is possible that he has been inactive since the arms. Both messages—'It took you long enough,' and especially, 'You'd have done better to leave me sleeping'—suggest very strongly that he had hoped for a reaction, some official response, back when he killed his victim, but has not killed since. Sometimes serial killers do lose the urge to kill. But now he is telling you that your sudden interest in the case has provoked him and reawakened his hunger."

"Great."

She stared hard at me. "It is not your fault, Detective Stone."

I nodded. "Dave's interest in the case at the time . . ."

"Is suggestive, but far from conclusive. I can tell you that two of your suspects, Peter and Dave, seem to fit, in general terms, a possible profile. But I would need to know a lot more about the crime, which of course is not possible, and you need to find out more about their backgrounds, their childhood relationships . . ."

Dehan sighed. "That makes a lot of sense."

I asked, "Can we come back to you as we learn more?"

"Of course, anytime." She smiled and handed me her card. "I'd be glad to hear from you."

Dehan blinked a lot and smiled. "What about me?"

Special Agent Fenninger smiled at her and rose to leave.

The door opened and a sergeant leaned in. "Detective Stone, you have a call on line one."

Fenninger smiled at Dehan. "It's okay, I'll see myself out."

"Thanks again!" I called to her neat, petite retreating form and picked up the phone. "Stone."

"Detective Stone, this is Detective Marco. I'm with the Sixty-Second Precinct, Rockaway Beach?" He said it like he was asking me.

I said, "Yeah."

"We are looking at a homicide that you may be interested in. We've got the crime scene guys in right now, but you might want to come down and have a look."

"Hank Junkers . . ."

"Uh-huh . . ."

TEN

THE GRAY DRIZZLE HAD TURNED TO HEAVY RAIN, WITH huge, broken clouds dragging in off the Atlantic like ripped sails from some cosmic Trafalgar. What traffic there was crawled through the cascades of rain with their lights splattered and distorted on the roads. It was half past one, but it looked more like early evening. I turned in to Hank's parking lot. It was cordoned off by yellow-and-black tape that was bouncing and dancing in the deluge. There was a meat wagon and a couple of cop cars, all with their red-and-blue lights, looking urgent and alarmed after the event. The third car belonged to Charles Hanlan, the ME.

We got out holding up our badges, ducked under the tape, and ran inside. The first thing I saw was Hank. He was lying more or less sideways against the door. His arms were splayed, like he'd fallen after a hefty blow to his head or his back. His legs were also splayed, as though he'd been standing akimbo. Stuck in his back, about where his heart was, was a dagger. It had been stabbed through a large piece of paper. Charles was squatting next to him, examining the back of his neck. He glanced up and muttered something as I stepped in.

The CSI guys looked as though they were finishing up.

Standing with his arms crossed in a long beige raincoat was the man I assumed was Detective Marco. He stepped toward me.

"You Stone?"

I showed him my badge and indicated Dehan. "Detective Dehan, my partner. What happened?"

"Kid from the neighborhood came to have his bicycle tire pumped up. Found him sprawled out like that. Ran, told his mom, and she called us."

"What made you call me?"

"Two things."

He reached in his pocket and pulled out an evidence bag. Inside the bag there was a cell phone. When he touched the screen, it lit up. It was open on the address book at my number.

"He was about to call me when he was killed."

"The phone had skidded over there, under that bike." He pointed at a bronze Harley 1200, two or three yards away from Hank's head. "The other thing is this." He stepped toward the body, and I followed him. "I noted your name, Stone. Take a look."

Dehan came up beside me, and we both looked down. There wasn't much blood on it, so it was easy to read. It said "STONE COLD."

I glanced at Charles. He was watching me. He had a way of looking at people that you learn in Harvard. "He was stabbed postmortem."

He nodded. "There is practically no bleeding. I'll be able to tell for sure when I get him back to the lab, but I am pretty certain what killed him was this blow to the back of the head. The bruising is extensive, and it feels as though it broke the vertebra."

Dehan asked the rookie question. "How long has he been dead?"

Charles patronized her with his best Harvard smile. "That's impossible to tell. Probably, *probably*, within the last seventy-two hours, because there is no immediate sign of decomposition."

"The blow"—I pointed at his neck—"was delivered from the

side." Charles raised an eyebrow at me. I continued, positioning myself behind where Hank had been standing. "If I hit him from here, the blow is going to be on the right side of his neck. It will stun him, but it probably won't kill him. But his bruise is straight across the back of his neck, which means that, if the killer was right-handed, he was standing there . . ." I moved to stand on Hank's left, round about where his feet were. "And I would strike like this, from the shoulder."

Charles was watching me and nodding. "Yes."

Marco scratched his chin. "What's your interest in this case, Stone?"

I was staring at the Harley. I said, absently, "It's probably related to an ongoing investigation. Does that strike you as strange?"

I pointed at the bike, and Dehan went and squatted down next to it. There was a neat, conical pile of sand directly in front of Hank's head. It made a perfect right angle with the center of the open door. I turned and looked behind me. There was a cement column, and at its base there was a heavy champagne bottle. The label had been soaked off, and it was full of water.

I pointed at it. "Two gets you twenty that's the murder weapon and . . ." I narrowed my eyes and stared at the ground about two yards behind Hank. "I am figuring, Detective Marco, that if you look just about there"—I pointed—"you are going to find traces of red wax."

He stared at me like I was crazy but went over, hunkered down, and looked anyway. He squinted, then pulled out his penknife and scraped at the floor. "Well, I'll be damned . . . How did you know that?"

"Believe it or not, Detective, this was a satanic ritual killing."

He made a "really?" face, and I heard Charles snort. I pointed at the bike. "North . . ."

Dehan took out her phone. I frowned. She had an app that was a compass. I sighed. She said, "Exactly north."

"Thank you. Earth, gold, wealth. You have the bike, the

greatest symbol of wealth to a Hells Angel, and you have a small pile of dirt." I pointed behind me. "West: water, emotion, the unconscious. The color green." I pointed at the bottle. "The weapon through which the killer's rage was expressed." I pointed across at the open door. "East: air, communication, the sword athame." I pointed at where the candle would have stood. "South: fire, red."

I stepped over by the door. "So, having knocked him down from the west, using water in a green bottle, I come over here and I take the dagger athame, and I use it to communicate my message by stabbing it into his back. Notice that the blade does not go, as you would expect, between the ribs, but it points north–south. Now . . ." I stood and took a few steps back. "Charles, in order to fall in that position, how would he have had to be standing? But let me ask you this, before you answer—to have his arms splayed like that, how much force would the blow have had to carry?"

He stood. He was nodding. "It's a very good point, John. A powerful rifle might do it. Or a Smith and Wesson Magnum. And he would have had to be standing in a very bizarre position, with his legs splayed."

Dehan was looking from Charles to me. "You're saying he was positioned after he was killed."

I nodded. "Yeah. What shape is he in?"

She stared at him. "A five-pointed star. A pentagram."

"Zak had several around his club."

Marco sighed loudly. "Is this your investigation, Stone?"

"I think so. I'll get my commander to call your precinct. I don't mind who has it, as long as you're willing to share your information. This man is probably dead because I questioned him about a cold case."

He was shaking his head. "I'll talk to the chief. You want it, you're welcome to it." He stepped away, dialing his precinct.

Charles was stripping off his gloves and closing his black bag. "You done with the body?"

"Yeah. You'll let me know if anything unexpected shows up?"

He saluted and left, and the guys brought in the gurney to take Hank away. Dehan watched them wheel him out and asked me, "Why do you know that?"

I stared at her a long time, like I was wondering whether to tell her something or not. Finally, I sighed and said, "There is an ancient mystery. It dates back to the fifteenth century, 1455, in Germany. Though it is said that the mystery is rooted in much older traditions that go back to ancient Japan and Korea . . ." I paused. She was watching me, waiting. I said, "Books. It's called books."

"Jerk. Why would you read a book on ritual magic? Athame, the north, gold, earth . . ."

I shrugged. "You start reading Freud, that leads you to Jung, next thing you know you're reading Kabbala. One thing leads to another."

The CSI team were bagging the bottle and the sand and dusting the bike for prints when Marco came back.

"We're happy to let you have it, Stone. My chief will call your chief, and we'll send over all the stuff. Take it easy."

I gave him a thumbs-up and he left. The CSI guys finally packed up and left too, and Dehan and I were left alone. I stood staring at the space where Hank had lain, trying to visualize what had happened.

Dehan spoke suddenly. "He must have brought the candle, the bottle, and the sand with him. He would have stepped in here . . ." She stood in the doorway, with the rain spattering behind her, looking in. "What did Hank say? How did he receive him?"

"He was scared."

"Because he pulled out his phone and started to call you, walking away, toward the bike. That means one thing. He recognized his killer as somebody dangerous, that you needed to know about."

"That's good."

"So is the killer alone? If it's two or three Angels, good luck finding anyone who noticed some bikers at a bike garage on a rainy day."

"Either way, he didn't run and it doesn't look like he put up a fight."

"So he was scared enough to call you, but not panicking or fighting for his life. For some reason he walks over there, toward the Harley." She paused. "Now that's important."

"Why?"

"Because the Harley is the right color for the north. I can't imagine that the killer brought a 1200 CC with him just to place it in the north end of the garage when he killed him. So we have to believe that the positioning of the bike was fortuitous. Which suggests a degree of opportunism. The killing pentacle was constructed around existing elements. The door for the air, the bike for the north."

I sighed and rubbed my face. A cold breeze crept in through the door and wheedled its way into my ankles.

"Ritual and note suggest a serial killer. But we are both thinking Zak—it all points to Zak, which would make it a motive killing, a punishment execution. And, also, as Fenninger said, Zak does not fit our profile."

We were silent a moment, and then she went on like I hadn't said anything.

"Hank moves toward the Harley, dialing your cell. As he does so, Zak, or whoever, moves across, taking out the bottle to place himself in the west, and smashes him in the back of the neck. Probably intending to stun him and not kill him. He, or they, then set him out in a pentagram, place the sand and the candle, move over to the east, and stab him with the knife, through the note. A note for you, to tell you you are cold, on the wrong track."

"It's rash," I said. "The door is wide open, and somebody could have turned up at any moment. It shows huge arrogance and recklessness. Also, as you say, he didn't know if Hank was dead. If he had been alive, the note would have been saturated and barely legible. It was not planned or carefully thought out."

"We are almost certainly looking at Zak for this."

We stared at each other for a long moment. Finally, I asked her, "Are we just reading a degree of planning and care into the placing of the arms, when really it was just a reckless act that paid off?" I shrugged at my own question and went and stood next to her, staring out at the concrete parking lot awash with water, covered in a mist of spray an inch deep. "He's killed Lynda in some half-assed ritual in the woods in Connecticut. He buries her, but in his crazed mind he has some sick joke going on, about how Hank must be"—I spread my hands and looked at her—"missing the arms of his lover . . ."

"Jesus . . ."

"So he brings him the arms of his lover. But by the time he gets here he is tired, hungover, whatever, and suddenly the idea of walking in on Hank and handing him Lynda's arms doesn't seem such a great idea. So he does the next best thing. He picks the lock on his lockup—or so he thinks—and leaves the arms there for him to find."

"It's persuasive, Stone. But, he rolls open the steel blind and sees boxes, not bikes."

"It's dark, he's tired, stoned. He just wants to sleep. He dumps them and goes."

A squad car arrived from the 43rd to seal up the premises, and we climbed in the Jag and headed off slowly into the deluge. After a while, Dehan did a funny kind of one-shouldered shrug and said, "I could buy that."

I didn't say anything. I was trying to imagine Zak in plastic boot covers writing out, "Well, it took you long enough . . ."

It wasn't easy.

WE STOPPED at an English pub on Coney Island Avenue. Everything was dark mahogany and brass, and they had an open fire burning. We took a small, round table by the window and sat in the silver light of the afternoon clouds. Dehan looked tired. I realized that I felt tired. I hadn't slept much in the last couple of days.

"I told Zak I was looking for Hank," I said suddenly. "I liked Hank. He was making a real effort to be a better person. That's something a lot of good people never do."

She studied my face for a moment. "You're not responsible, Stone. You did what you had to do, the best you could."

"I know."

She smiled. "You're always telling me to think like a crook. With Zak you need to think like a psychopath, or a sociopath. He didn't care whether Hank had shopped him or not. He might have. That was enough."

"Yup. I should have seen that."

She pulled a face. "And what? Would you have done any different? Hank took his chances. He rode with the Devil, and he got burned."

We chinked glasses.

"We haven't got enough to pull him in. We have to wait for forensics. In the meantime, we need to find out more about Pete, and especially Dave."

She nodded. "You don't think the arms are Lynda's, do you?"

"I can't make up my mind. It makes sense that they are. It makes sense that Zak killed her, and it makes sense that he planted the arms there as some kind of sick joke. But I can't shake the feeling that there is somebody else, totally different, standing in the shadows watching."

She chuckled. "Somebody who would write"—she put on a prissy voice and waggled her head and her bum—"'Well, it took you long enough!'"

I laughed. "You read my mind. It just doesn't sound like Zak."

I had ordered two burgers, and the waitress brought them over. We ate hungrily and in silence. After a while, she said, "You want me to take Peter?"

I nodded. "Yeah, I want to have a good look at Dave."

ELEVEN

I called GCS, Dave's company, and asked to be put through to the MD. The girl on reception said she'd put me through to Mr. Fischer, the owner and managing director. He agreed to see me that afternoon.

The Global Computer Shipping Company was somewhat smaller than its name suggested, and was located on the top floor of a brown, two-story building on East Tremont Avenue, about ten minutes' walk from the lockup. I climbed a narrow staircase, carpeted in the same brown as the walls, and stepped into a large, brown reception area. The receptionist looked at me sadly as I approached her desk and asked me, "Mister, is it *ever* going to stop raining?"

I smiled cheerfully and said, "Yup, the day I get a Facebook account."

"*Please* get a Facebook account . . ."

"Never!"

She wheezed like I was the funniest man in the world and asked me, "You the cop?" She picked up the internal phone and pressed a button. "Mr. Fischer, Detective Stone is here to see you . . . Okay . . ." She pointed at a door and said, "Right through there."

I knocked and went in. It was a large room paneled in wood, with large windows overlooking a wet street where everybody seemed to be leaning forward under umbrellas. Fischer stood to greet me. He was in his early sixties with tightly curled gray hair and a pencil moustache of the sort that was fashionable back in the '50s. He was slim, and his clothes were on the flash side of elegant. He shook my hand and gestured me to a chair.

"Detective Stone," he said as he sat. "How can we help you?"

"I was hoping you could give me some information on one of your employees?"

His eyebrows shot up. "Really? Which one? Is he in trouble?"

I held his eye a moment and asked him, "Do you not employ women?"

He smiled, sighed, and sat back. "We have a small staff, Detective, and I know them all very well. I am afraid there is only one of them who is likely to attract the attention of the police. It's David, isn't it?"

"David Hansen."

He nodded. "He is my nephew. This company exists for him and because of him."

I frowned. "How's that?"

"His father, my sister's husband, died when David was a very small boy, barely two years old. I created this company as a way to provide for them. What do you want to know about him? Is it the pornography again?"

I shook my head. "Not exactly." I hadn't expected this, and I wasn't sure how best to proceed. He must have seen the uncertainty on my face, because he said, "It's all right, Detective. We are a very religious family, and my first loyalty is to God. If he has done wrong, I will not shield him."

I hesitated. "I believe he goes away occasionally, to information technology conferences . . ."

"Yes. As I told you"—he gestured with both hands at the office around him—"this company was created for him, and by him. We realized at an early age that David was . . ." He thought carefully about the word. "*Special*. He was diagnosed with moderate to severe dyspraxia, dyslexia, and mild autism. He has a very high IQ, bordering on genius, but he can come across as, well, frankly, dumb. Stupid. As you can imagine, all of these things make it very difficult for him to relate to people, and he suffered a great deal at school. He got very poor grades and did not go to university. University would have destroyed him."

I figured he would eventually get around to answering my question. In the meantime, I was interested in what he was telling me. He thought for a moment, like he was imagining his nephew being destroyed at university, then went on.

"His great passion, from a very early age, was computers. I guess they provided him with a world where he felt safe, and he could communicate with people in a way where he did not feel threatened. So I paid for him to have private tuition, and eventually he went to a technical college and became qualified as, I don't know what. I, personally, know nothing about computers. This is why I say that *he* created this company as much as I did." He laughed like he'd made a joke and continued. "He passed all his exams with flying colors, and when I saw how good he was, and how *dedicated*, I started GCS. I started him at the bottom, and he is working his way up.

"Now, twice a year, as regular as clockwork, he attends these conferences where they exhibit the latest technology, give talks, discuss the latest research . . ." He made a "and so on" gesture with his hand. "And very properly, David attends these conferences."

"Where are these conferences held? Is it always the same place, or does the venue change?"

He was shaking his head before I had finished. Outside there was a roll of thunder, and a sudden squall of rain on the window made him glance outside.

"San Diego in the summer. It's always the third weekend in July, Thursday to Sunday. And the first weekend in December in Los Angeles."

"So on December 5, 2005, he had just come back from Los Angeles."

He looked surprised. "I have no idea. That was twelve years ago. But if it was a Monday, then yes. As far as I am aware, he has never missed one yet." He smiled. "He is also somewhat OCD."

"How does he travel? Does he go by plane?"

"By train or car. He doesn't like to fly." He frowned suddenly. "Forgive me, Detective, but these are rather peculiar questions. Do you mind telling me what this is about?"

I felt suddenly weary and gazed out at the interminable gray rain and drizzle. I asked myself the same question. What *was* it all about? I sighed and said, "I wish I knew, Mr. Fischer." Then, "We're looking into the background and movements of a number of people who have a connection to the lockups at the back of Revere Avenue."

"The lockups . . . Why on Earth . . . ?"

"My next question may seem a little odd, Mr. Fischer."

"They all seem a little odd, to be frank, Detective."

"Would you say that David has a good relationship with his mother?"

His face flushed and his eyes shone. "What are you implying, Detective?"

"I'm not implying anything. I am asking you. I am trying to eliminate David from a list of possible suspects."

"Suspects in what? Why won't you tell me?"

"Twelve years ago, a woman's arms were found in one of the units in that alley. The case went cold, and now we are reviewing it. David is one of a number of people we are looking into."

His face, which had flushed red, now turned ashen. "I remember that case. You can't possibly think David . . . He wasn't even here . . ."

"We are looking into the possibility that the murder was committed somewhere else."

He stood and walked to the window. "My God . . . David . . ."

I gave him a moment, then said, "He is just one of a number

of people we are—" I hesitated. "—trying to eliminate from our inquiry."

He turned and stared at me. "Yes . . . yes, of course. Eliminate from . . . As I said, he was not a happy child." He returned to his chair and sat carefully, as though sitting quickly might somehow have made David guilty of murder. "His mother was—*is*—naturally, protective. Perhaps a little too much so, but there is nothing . . ." He glanced at me. "Nothing *untoward* or *unhealthy* in their relationship." I went to speak, but he rushed on. "I can *vouch* for the fact that he was never in any way abused as a child. In *any way* at all!"

I nodded. For some reason, I had suddenly had enough of Fischer and his weird family. I went to stand and said, "Can you tell me the name of these conferences that David goes to? Or the venue?"

He shook his head. "I would have to ask him."

"Your accounts department must have records . . ."

He shook his head. "No, he pays for them himself. You want me to ask him now?"

"No. It's okay. Probably best if you don't mention my visit. In all probability, he will be eliminated anyway."

"Yes . . . You think so?"

I stood and held out my hand. "Thanks for your help, Mr. Fischer."

The lights were starting to come on as I climbed into my car and closed the door. The air was a grainy dusk touched with wet amber and red. I sat, drumming the wheel and watching the dark close in. I fired up the engine and drove slowly the short distance back to the precinct. By the time I got there, it was dark.

Dehan looked up from her laptop and watched me sit down. We sat staring at each other for a while. It was a comfortable habit we had gotten into. When I switched on my computer, she returned to her research. After half an hour, I leaned back and said, "Dave is lying to his uncle."

Her eyes peered at me over the top of her screen. I explained about my meeting with Fischer and then pointed at my computer. "I have scoured Google with every variation and permutation of IT conferences, and there are no major computer conferences that occur regularly on the third weekend of July and the first weekend of December."

"You going to ask him where he's been going for the past twelve years?"

"Not yet. I want to know the answer before I ask him. See if he lies."

"We haven't got enough for a warrant to see his bank and credit card records."

"I know . . . Another couple of weeks and we could follow him. But something tells me we haven't got a couple of weeks."

I picked up my phone and called Bernie at the bureau.

"Stone. What can I do for you?"

"Hey, Bernie. I need a favor . . ." I explained the situation to him and concluded, "I know you cannot check his bank records and credit card without a warrant, so I am not asking you to do that . . . but I was thinking you might be able to come up with a creative idea, because I know in my bones that this killer is building up to another kill. You hearing me . . . ?"

"Yeah, I'm hearing you, John. Email me his details, and I'll give it some thought and get back to you."

"Appreciate it, Bernie."

Dehan was watching me with no expression at all. Behind her the window looked very black.

"You just asked a special agent to break the law."

"You misheard. I specifically asked him not to. How are you doing?"

"I can certainly add to your general state of confusion, if that's what you mean. I have been trawling through what is available in public records, and Peter has an interesting past."

"Oh, God . . ."

"He was orphaned at the age of four. Witnessed both his parents killed in a robbery. They were both knifed. He was adopted at the age of five, and eleven years later, at the age of sixteen, he left home and started working, doing menial jobs—burger joints, shop assistant, that kind of thing. Got his driver's license at seventeen and at eighteen got his job as a sales rep for Canadian American Chemicals. Progressed rapidly. Married Jenny at twenty-one and that same year took out a mortgage on the house he now owns."

"Okay . . ."

"There is more. He attended St. Mary's Catholic School, primary and secondary. I managed to track down one of his teachers—still works at the school—and I went over and had a chat with him."

"Good work. What did you find out?"

"Don't interrupt. He remembered Peter very well. He said the staff were all aware that he was adopted and that he had had a very traumatic experience. The parents were supposed to take him to a child psychologist on a regular basis, once a week, and for the first couple of years they did, and he seemed to be doing okay. He was a shy, timid child, but he was making friends, and the teachers kept an eye on him to make sure there was no bullying and that kind of stuff.

"But he said, around the time Peter turned eight, things started to go wrong at home. Word from the other parents was that Dad had started drinking heavily. Peter started missing days at school. When he did turn up, Mom sometimes had bruises. Teachers tried talking to her, she got mad, told them to mind their own business—the usual shit. When Peter started turning up with bruises, they contacted social services, who looked into it and concluded there was not enough evidence to do anything. A visit to the house apparently showed it to be clean, and both parents were sober and seemed happy. The kid was shy, but that was to be expected. He had stopped going to the psychologist, but the parents were under no obligation to take him if they deemed him to be okay."

"That explains why he left home at sixteen."

"Yup."

I rubbed my eyes. Brilliant drops of water were trickling down the black glass behind Dehan's head. For some reason, they were making me sleepy. I really wanted to go home and sleep. I sighed. "We have to start eliminating suspects."

She gave a humorless laugh. "You may want to rephrase that. And speaking of which, the lab phoned. The soap was mixed with chicken's blood. There were no prints anywhere. The shoe print on your mat would be a man of about five ten to six foot. The tread belongs to a fairly uncommon shoe. It's European, and you'd have to buy it online or go to Europe." She was leafing through pages in her notebook. "Gallardo. A Spanish shoe. Hand-made, real leather, they have a website—gallardo.com."

I typed it in and looked at their shoes. They were nice. I memorized the tread.

"Maybe, Dehan, maybe at last we have something."

TWELVE

I dropped Dehan at her apartment and then passed by the shopping mall to get a bottle of Floradix liquid iron. When I got home, I checked the back door was bolted, poured some liquid iron into a tumbler, and went out on the porch. The road was silent but for the gentle patter of drizzle on the leaves. Nothing moved except the leaves of the evergreens bowing gently in the icy breeze. The gleam of the streetlamps on the wet blacktop gave it a feeling of desolation. I wondered if he was out there, watching me. I carried my glass down to the sidewalk and stood looking first one way, then the other, scanning the small front gardens, identifying each car by owner. There was nothing I could see that was out of the ordinary.

I went back up the steps to the porch, where the door stood open. I smelled the liquid iron. It was awful. I bent and carefully spilled it all over the porch. Then I went inside to make myself a steak and sleep the sleep of the babes and angels.

I was in bed by ten, and by four seconds past, I was asleep. I slept deeply and solidly for five hours. At three I woke up, and for a couple of seconds I wasn't sure if I was dreaming or not. My front doorbell was ringing incessantly. I heard a car door slam and the rising pitch of a car pulling away, then fading. I pulled on my pants, slipped my automatic in my waistband, and went downstairs. There was a note on the mat, and the bell was still ringing.

I cocked the gun, stood to one side, removed the chair, and opened the door. Nothing happened. The bell was still ringing. I peered outside. There was nobody on the porch and nobody visible in the street. There was a toothpick wedged in the bell. I pulled it out and the ringing stopped. I examined it to see if it had been chewed. It hadn't.

I closed the door, got my surgical gloves from my jacket pocket, and picked up the note. I sat in my armchair and read it.

WELL, Detective Stone, here we are at last. It has been a long time coming. I confess I had given up. Your colleagues twelve years ago were anything but persistent. They were no mach for me and, ironically, I found that demoralizing. That bestial hunger, that daemon that dwells within me, fell into a long slumber. But now I realize it was simply waiting for it's moment of destiny, an opponant worthy of my genius. And here you are, finally, ready to do battle. I shall not disappoint you.

The Beast is awake and hungry, be prepared.

I READ it over several times, assimilating the elaborate wordiness, the slightly infantile attempt at archaic English, the misspelling of "match" and "opponent," and the misused apostrophe in "its." I scanned it and saved a copy on my computer, printed a copy, and put the original in an evidence bag, then called the precinct for a crime scene team to come over.

They arrived fifteen minutes later, and after I'd chatted with Frank—the team leader—for five minutes, I told them to help themselves to coffee and lock up when they were done. Then I sent Dehan a WhatsApp telling her I wouldn't pick her up in the morning, and went back to bed to sleep another four hours.

Next morning, I had a couple of messages waiting for me

when I got to my desk. The first was an email from the San Diego PD, with several attachments. Detective Ramirez had heard that I was looking into unsolved dismemberment cases and had remembered one from the summer of 2005. He had taken the trouble to dig it out and send it to me.

I printed it and read through it. There wasn't much. Some workmen had found a torso in the wasteland near the MCAS Miramar airfield. It was female, and the arms, legs, and head had been removed. As with our arms, whoever had done it had some skill, though not perhaps the skill of a surgeon. The rest of the body was never found. There was practically no forensic evidence, and they were never able to go any further with it.

I looked at the date. The torso was found Monday, July 18. Exact time of death was impossible to determine, but decomposition was in its earliest stages. The body being out in the open air, that would suggest it had been there only a very short time.

I checked the calendar for 2005. I didn't need to, but it pays to be thorough. The eighteenth was the Monday following the third weekend.

The second message was from the sheriff of Lyman County in South Dakota. He didn't know if it would be of any interest to me or not, but a few years back, 2012, they had found some human remains just outside Oacoma. It seemed to be a woman's skull. Judging by the work that had been done on her teeth, it was a modern skull. By the state of decomposition, she had been dead several years. But that was about all they could determine. I sat and stared at the window and wondered if the weather was any better in South Dakota than it was in New York.

My phone rang. It was Dehan.

"You awake yet?"

"No, this is my answering service. Where are you?"

"I'm at the lab. You should come over."

"I'm on my way."

Half an hour later, I left my car in the parking lot and met Dehan outside the lab. She looked at me curiously.

"You okay?"

"Sure. What's he got?"

"I'll let him tell you."

Frank looked at me and grunted as we walked in. "I am no expert," he said, "but if you want this man for an organized serial killer, you had better start looking elsewhere. It is possible, of course, that he is becoming overconfident, but . . ." He shook his head and pulled a face, as though he didn't like what he'd just said.

He walked over to the table where he had the bottle, the knife, and the note laid out. He pointed at the bottle and said, "He didn't wear gloves. What he did was wipe the weapons clean after the killing. My impression . . ." And he paused here to stare at me for a moment. "My *impression* is that he was so excited by the killing that he couldn't be bothered to be careful."

I frowned. "Hence the enormous strength of the blow that was meant to stun him but actually killed him."

"Exactly. I don't know if you noticed the wet footprints?" I shook my head. He shrugged. "By the time you got there they had probably been trampled over, but we photographed them. If you study the photographs, I would say he actually ran, doing side-steps like a tennis player, as the victim walked away from him"—he mimicked the action, with both fists closed as though he were holding a racket, or a bottle by the neck—"and gave him an almighty double-handed backhander that smashed his vertebra and broke his neck."

"So did you recover anything?"

He held up a hand. "Wait. I am making a point here, John. He left partials on the bottle and on the knife. But he obviously thought, as most people do, that you can't leave a print on paper. Actually, paper is an excellent surface for leaving prints because it absorbs sweat and oil from the pores. You apply disulfur dinitride and the print comes up brown. Voila . . ." He led me to the note that had been pinned to Hank's back. It was covered in clear prints. "They are being run through IAFIS as we speak."

"That's good news. That's very good news."

"Hmmm . . ." He didn't sound convinced. "But you have a problem, John. Compare that behavior with your visitor from last night." He led me over to the other note. "The *only* prints on this paper are yours. This paper was handled with surgical gloves from the moment it came out of the pack, to the moment you picked it up."

I looked at Dehan. "That is conclusive as far as I am concerned. We are dealing with two different people."

She was nodding. "Zak and somebody else."

Frank said, "Somebody very careful and very meticulous."

"Though not about their spelling."

He smiled. "No, not about their spelling."

An assistant poked his head around the door and said, "We have a hit on the prints, Frank." He handed him a piece of paper. Frank glanced at it and handed it to me. Dehan came and looked over my shoulder.

She murmured, "Zachariah Brunell. Wanted on multiple charges of assault, assault with a deadly weapon, rape . . . the list goes on. Wanted in thirty out of fifty states, but not in Maine. Not in New England."

There was a mug shot. It was Zak. I nodded. "Well, now he is wanted for murder."

I called the precinct and had the lieutenant contact the Maine PD and send a couple of cars out to the Hellfire Club, though I was pretty certain Zak wouldn't be there. So I had him put out an APB too.

WE SAT IN THE CAFETERIA, looking out at the rain falling steadily in the parking lot. I told Dehan about my visitor and the two emails.

"I thought we could go to South Dakota. If we take it in turns to drive, we can do it in a day."

She nodded.

"Something tells me this could be the head that belongs to the arms."

She nodded again. "But it's not Lynda. Lynda is out in Connecticut, probably in the lake where they had their rally."

"We could take a small detour on the way back from Oacoma."

She chuckled. "Small."

"We can ask Dutchess County to drag the lake, but I'd like to have a look first."

"Sure. So who are we looking at, Stone?"

"You notice the spelling? So meticulous about everything else, but sloppy in his spelling."

"I also noticed the rather grandiose language. You know what it reminded me of? Gamers."

"Gamers?"

"Yeah, they play online computer games. They take on the identity of some dragon-slayer hero from some fantasy universe like *Conan the Barbarian* or *Lord of the Rings*, and they go on quests and do battle with orcs and dragons and all that shit."

"Computer fantasies . . ." I thought for a moment. "Fischer said that Dave suffered from dyspraxia and dyslexia."

"We need to find out where Dave was in July 2005. The date fits, third weekend of July. But where? No word from Bernie, huh?"

I sighed and glanced at my watch. "You need to collect a toothbrush?"

She shook her head. "I can pick one up on the way."

"So, let's go."

THIRTEEN

THE WEATHER IN SOUTH DAKOTA IN NOVEMBER IS VERY cold, but there were at least broken clouds, and it was a relief to see patches of blue among the gray. We crossed the bridge over the Missouri, from Chamberlain to Oacoma, at eleven the next morning. I had called ahead and arranged to meet Sheriff Pete Marlow at Al's Oasis at eleven thirty, but he was already there drinking coffee when we arrived.

He was a big man with a beard and an easy smile. He offered us coffee, but I said I'd like to see where the skull was found, and the skull itself. He gave that smile that says "city folks is always in a hurry" and led us out to his Ford pickup.

We clambered in and he glanced at Dehan in the mirror. "It ain't far. Shoot! Nothin's far in Oacoma." We crossed the I-90 and drove through the town. It was leafy and quiet, and sometimes you could imagine you were not in a town at all, but driving through open parkland. We crossed over a small rail track and turned onto Gilbert Avenue, and then took a dirt track down onto rolling green slopes that were dotted with occasional copses. He drove to the top of a small hill and stopped.

"We'll walk it from here," he said. "It's about three or four hundred yards down, through them woods."

There was an icy wind sweeping down from the north. It clawed its way through your clothes and bit into your skin. I saw Dehan wince and shudder as she pulled her hair from her face.

We were in a small delta valley. On my left, I could see the Missouri about a hundred and fifty yards away, huge, slow, and green, snaking past. Ahead of us, at the bottom of the valley, was a dense woodland that said there was a creek down there, feeding the trees with water on its way down to the big river. As if to confirm my thoughts, the sheriff pointed down and said, "That there is the North Fork Creek, runs down to the river yonder. That's where we found it."

We started to walk down the slope toward the woods, with condensation billowing from our mouths as though we were all smoking cigarettes. Dehan asked, "Who found it?"

"It was a family out walking their dogs. It's nice 'round here, and the town folk like to go out in the evening or on the weekend. It was the dog found it, in the creek. God knows how long it had been there."

The trees had grown dense, and you could hear the sound of water running and splashing below. Finally, we came out onto a narrow riverbank. The creek was maybe twenty feet across and fast flowing. Marlow pointed upstream.

"We figured maybe the body was upstream. If it wasn't buried, the coyotes would get to it, and if the head come loose, maybe the water carried it down. We went up and searched. We took a couple of dogs, but we never found anything."

I asked him, "Did you look downstream too?"

"Yup, but we never found anything there, neither. Plus, when the boys at the lab had a look, they said she hadn't decomposed in water. There was very little sign of water erosion on the skull. They said their best guess was that the skull had only been in water for a short while. What a short while was, they didn't care to say."

I pointed upstream, where he had pointed moments before.

"So if I follow this creek back up that way, I will eventually come to the I-90 . . ."

"Yup. You got three bridges side by side. You got the eastbound and the westbound, and then you got Highway 16. They all cross over the creek at the same point."

Dehan was breathing into her hands and said, "The I-90 is going to take you all the way to Seattle. But before you get there, you are going to come to Butte, where the I-15 is going to take you south all the way to San Diego MCAS Miramar."

The sheriff looked at her like she might be crazy, but he was too polite to say so. I said, "What are you, an atlas?"

She shrugged. "I know my roads."

I turned to the sheriff. "Can we see the skull?"

He began making his way back up the slope through the trees. "I figured you'd want to. It's in the truck. I made you a copy of the file we have on it. It ain't much, but it's all what there is."

We got back to the truck, and he yanked open the back. There was a blue-and-white cooler, which he opened and withdrew a cardboard box from. From that, he extracted a human skull. It gave me a frenzied grin which, oddly, was devoid of all humor because the eyes were dark and hollow. The jaw was still attached, but when I tipped the skull back I could see there had been some dental work done.

I asked him, "Were any attempts made to extract DNA?"

He shook his head. "We haven't got many resources, Detective Stone. There was nobody missing from my county, nor any of the neighboring counties."

"Sure. Can I borrow the skull? I can get my commander to submit a formal request . . ."

"I've already prepared the paperwork. All you have to do is sign the receipt. Ain't no darn use to me, and if you can find out who the poor girl was and give her family some peace, I figure it's more use to you than me."

We took care of the paperwork and then went and checked in at the Oasis Inn. There was a cute parade of shops whose fronts were made out to look like old Western buildings, but inside they were the same prefab shops you'd find in New York or Los Angeles. Dehan stood staring at them awhile and said, "It makes you wonder, doesn't it, Stone? They had the originals, they got rid of the originals, and then made fakes to look like the originals they got rid of." I smiled and she started walking toward Al's Oasis. "What will they do next century, do you think? Will they make fake fakes to look like the real fakes we have now?"

"Probably."

We had a couple of buffalo burgers and beer and sat by the window. It was good to see patches of sunlight on green grass, and blue sky through broken clouds.

"After lunch we'll go over the river to Chamberlain and have the skull sent to the forensic anthropologist. I figure there might just be enough material to get some DNA. If the head and the arms prove to be the same person, we'll be getting somewhere."

She chewed and thought. "So, we have a rough sketch of somebody who maybe has a route from San Diego, via South Dakota, to New York. Who selects victims at random, young women, kills them, dismembers them, and then distributes their body parts along the route."

"It's possible, yes."

"He is a narcissistic fantasist who is probably obsessed with *Conan the Barbarian*-type computer games and can't spell." I finished my buffalo burger and nodded. "It is beginning to sound a lot like Dave. Two gets you twenty, Dave has been visiting San Diego in July and some other Californian location in December."

I was still nodding as I wiped my mouth. "It certainly looks that way."

That was when my phone rang. It was Bernie.

"Bernie, tell me you have some good news."

"I have news, John, I don't know if you are going to consider it good. Also, bear in mind you cannot use this in court because it was not legally obtained."

"I know, Bernie. Tell me what you've got." I put it on speaker and laid the phone on the table.

"You couldn't find where your suspect was going because there are no such conferences. For the dates you're talking about, every year for the past fourteen years he has been attending, in July, the San Diego Comic and Sci-Fi Fantasy Convention, and in December, the Fantasy Gamers' Convention in Los Angeles."

For a moment, I felt oddly depressed. I said, without much feeling, "That is perfect, Bernie. Where has he been staying? Is it always the same hotel?"

"Hold your horses there, pal. That is by no means the whole story. Because while he has been enjoying the events of the conventions during the day, by night he has been enjoying a very different kind of entertainment."

I frowned. "Really? Like what?"

"In San Diego he goes nightly, like clockwork, to the Bull Rhino Club on Mission Gorge, at a cost of two hundred bucks a night. And in L.A. he goes to the Angels Massage Parlor on Olympic Boulevard."

"So, twice a year he gets away to satisfy his fantasies without his mother or his uncle knowing about it."

"That's what it looks like, John."

"Thanks, Bernie. That is really helpful. Take it easy."

"Sure thing. One more thing you might be interested to know. For the last thirteen years, he's been seeing a psychoanalyst twice a month."

He hung up and Dehan and I sat staring at each other. What else could we do?

FOURTEEN

WE WERE BOTH EXHAUSTED, SO WE DIDN'T DISCUSS IT anymore. After dispatching the skull, we went back to the motel. I left her at her room, showered, and slept until six. There is something disconcerting about going to bed when it's light and waking up when it's dark. I lay for a while staring into the darkness above me and wondering where I was and if anybody had left me a note.

Then memories came back. The skull. David. The brothels. I put on the light, had a shower to wake myself up, and got dressed, thinking of Al's Oasis and the eight-ounce sirloins I had seen on the menu.

I knocked on Dehan's door, and she came out with wet hair and a big smile on her face. She put a silver pendant on a chain in my hand and turned her back to me, lifting her hair up to expose her neck. "Put it on me, will you?"

I looked at it. It was a David's star with an inscription on the back. It said, *To Carmen Dehan, from Mom and Daddy, on her first birthday, May 9, 1991.*

We had an awkward moment as I slipped it around her neck. Then I did it up, and she dropped her hair over my hands. I wiped them dry on my pants, and we walked the short distance across the parking lot in silence. She gave me a sudden, mischievous grin and said, "You know? This is the closest I ever get to going on a date."

I raised an eyebrow at her and smiled. It was the closest I ever got too, but I wasn't going to tell her that. Instead I said, "Yeah? Why?"

She shrugged. "I hate people. People hate me."

"I don't think people hate you, Dehan. You're actually a . . ." I hesitated. "A really *nice* person. But people are terrified of your attitude. If you just toned down the attitude a bit . . ."

She was still smiling, but she looked curious. As I pulled open the door, she said, "Does it bother you?"

I followed her in and surprised myself by saying, "No, I kind of like it."

A gleaming waitress with gleaming teeth and hair smiled at us and said, "Table for two?"

She led us to a table for two, and we ordered two beers and two steaks. As we sat, I said, "You're attractive, you're intelligent, you're funny—there must be lots of men out there who'd . . ."

She cut across me with, "I'm good."

"You're good?"

"I'm good."

I grinned. "Okay . . ." And we both laughed for no particular reason. We followed the laugh with an awkward silence, and Dehan said suddenly, "So what's next?"

"You mean after our date?"

"Cut it out." But she was still smiling.

I shrugged. "I guess we call David in and have a chat with him. Ask him how come he's been lying to his uncle for the last twelve years. I'd also like to talk to his shrink, but that won't be easy."

She was quiet for a bit, turning the saltcellar around in circles.

"If he thinks you and he have this special connection, you could play on that. He probably couldn't resist the temptation to engage in some kind of heroes' repartee with you."

I watched her but didn't say anything. After a moment, she raised her eyes to mine, narrowed them, and sat back.

"Son of a bitch."

I smiled.

"You don't think he did it."

I made a face like brain constipation and said, "I wouldn't go that far. I'm just not satisfied yet."

"Come on, Stone. This is just being contrary. What more do you want? He fits the bill in every respect. He was *there*, for crying out loud."

"So were one and a half million other people."

"Come on!"

"Okay, here's my problem. He was going to brothels. Everything else rings true, but *that* strikes a false note. This murder, or murders, is all about frustration, about pent-up rage that the killer can't release. He should be sitting at home watching porn, not spending two hundred dollars a night getting laid in a brothel."

"Since when are you a psychologist?"

"Fair point, but still, it feels wrong."

The steaks came and the gleaming waitress instructed us to enjoy them. Dehan cut into hers and put the first slice into her mouth. She gave a gentle sigh and waved her fork at me, raising an eyebrow.

"I am going to tell you what you would tell me. You are making assumptions." She was right, and I said so. "For starters, you are assuming that he is going to these whorehouses and shagging his brains out every night, but I am going to put two scenarios to you."

"Okay."

"Scenario one . . ." She cut another piece of steak and stuck it in her mouth, talking with her mouth full. "He spends all day living out his fantasy as some legendary, barbarian superhero or supervillain. He builds up in his mind this *unrealizable* image of himself. And by the evening he is ready to go not whoring, but *wenching*. But when he gets to the whorehouse, what happens? He can't get it up. Because he can't get it up with real, hot, flesh-and-blood women. He can only get it up with a two-dimensional virtual woman who doesn't threaten him. And every time that happens, his rage builds a little more, until on the fourth day he can't take it anymore and he goes out, finds a suitable victim, probably a street whore, and kills her in a manner befitting a wild barbarian but chopping her into pieces."

I sipped my beer. "That is a very credible scenario."

"Scenario two." She leveled her knife at me. "What I just described happened twelve and thirteen years ago. But he's been seeing his shrink. And the shrink has encouraged him to live out his fantasies and try to make them real, keep it secret from his mom and his uncle so that they will not judge him, and have as many whores as he can manage. And he says to him, 'Don't worry about not getting it up, pal, because I will give you some tablets that, when you take them, will give you a hard-on worthy of a titan. And you will be the hero of the night. You will give those wenches the ride of their lives!' And what happens?" She spread her hands. "You were right. It works. He stops killing."

I made a face of deep respect. "That is a very compelling argument, Detective Dehan."

"For twelve years. Until you come along and upset the applecart."

We ate in silence for a bit. Finally, I said, "You know what? We dug into Dave, and look what we found. We'll pull him in, and we'll interrogate him. But for the sake of completeness, let's dig into Peter too and see what we find. If it's one or the other of them, it will become clear."

She shrugged one shoulder. "I guess."

She finished her steak and signaled the waitress, who came gleaming back to us with her teeth and her hair. Dehan smiled at her and said, "This is what I am going to do now. I am going to have an espresso coffee and a glass of Irish whiskey, which you are going to serve to me with no ice and in a cognac glass."

The waitress smiled and blinked a lot and said, "Okay!"

It seemed like a good idea, so I said I would do the same.

When she had gone away to fetch the goods, Dehan said, "So how about you, Stone, why don't you date?"

"Who says I don't?"

She made a face like a chipmunk and went, "Pffff!"

I shrugged. "I don't hate people. But I guess I don't really trust people. Maybe people sense that and they steer clear of me. I don't know. Either way, people and I—we don't really jibe."

The coffees and the whiskeys came, and I smiled. "I guess that makes us like Statler and Waldorf. You are Statler, I'm Waldorf."

We chinked glasses.

"Here's to that."

WE SET OUT EARLY, before the dawn, and drove all day, taking it in turns to sleep and drive. It was a tedious journey, mostly just a straight line along the I-90, through rain and drizzle, as far as Wisconsin. At Lake Erie, we stopped at a motel outside Toledo and had four hours' sleep, then continued on up. We got to Danbury at midnight, booked in to a motel, and went straight to bed. The next morning, after an early breakfast at seven, we drove out to Holmes, found Camp Road, and wound our way through woodlands to the lake at Camp Kaufmann.

We got there at shortly after eight. Most of the trees were tall and spindly, naked against the frozen gray sky. The water looked black and icy, and the ground was muddy from the relentless rain and drizzle. There was a patch of grass surrounded by huts, with a few canoes scattered here and there, and a long, wooden jetty reaching out into the water. The whole thing was enclosed by trees. I could see why Zak would have favored a place like this.

Dehan walked out onto the jetty and stood staring at the trees and the obsidian water. I watched her from the shore. Now that we were here, I wasn't sure what to do. After a moment I joined her, and we both turned to look back at the collection of huts. Dehan wiped the drizzle from her eyes and said, "She's here, isn't she?"

I could visualize the bikes. How many? Maybe thirty, forty, fifty of them. And a hundred Angels with their ladies. There would have been crates of beer, whiskey, tequila. There would have been music, mainly old music, evocative of the golden age: Van Morrison, Zeppelin, the Eagles. And there would have been a lot of weed and coke. And once Hank left, there would have been Lynda, sentenced to death and not knowing it. I said, "Probably."

"Where did he do it? Right here? Or did he take her away, into the woods?"

I pointed to a long spit that curled out into the lake and opened up into a patch of grass maybe thirty or forty feet across. "He did it right there, while they all watched."

We walked back and followed the long tongue of land out into the black water. There would have been a big fire burning on the bank. They would all have followed him down, a hundred black silhouettes against the flames, standing, watching, laughing, probably not knowing yet how it was going to end. And Zak would have performed his rough and ready ritual, as he had with Hank. I pointed to the left.

"The lake provides the water in the west."

I walked up to the northernmost point. It was still there. I hunkered down, and Dehan came and joined me. It was a crude circle of rocks that had been filled in with earth. As I gently moved away the sand, the remains of a yellow candle appeared, burned down and melted into the earth for the last twelve years. "Earth in the north."

I turned, and Dehan stood. "In that case," she said, "there should be something back there, in the south. Red, fire, right?"

I followed her back. There was another circle of rocks, three or four feet across, blackened by fire, neglected for over a decade.

"And in the east?"

"The air. And probably a blue candle."

"It must have been cold!"

I shrugged. "Part of the ordeal? Too drunk and stoned to notice? Who knows? But he had sex with her right there, in the center, and then probably stabbed her in the heart. What would he do then?"

We both stared at the lake. She pushed her wet hair out of her face. "Weighted down with rocks? They couldn't have got her very deep—the water would have been icy. It would have made more sense to bury her."

"Maybe they did both. What's that?" I walked to the center of the area where Zak had made his temple. "The pentagram represents the head of a goat. The two horns would be there and there." I pointed northeast and northwest. "Its beard would be behind me in the south. That rock is dead center, between the horns, and if I'm not mistaken, there is something painted on it."

The rock was half in the water, balanced on a slope where the bank dipped down to the lake. It was about three feet across and roughly spherical. As we approached, we saw that it had, indeed, a faded cross painted on it. But the cross was upside down. I felt a sudden rush of irrational urgency, like I needed to get Lynda out of that place, that it was somehow important. I dropped on my knees and began to dig. Dehan ran, but I ignored her.

After a couple of minutes she came back, carrying two canoe paddles. Between us, we levered away the rock, wiping the water from our eyes, until suddenly it gave and rolled into the lake with a big splash. Then we used the paddles as spades and began to dig. It wasn't a deep grave. They were too drunk, cold, and probably wet to make the effort. She was only about two feet down. The damp earth had not preserved her. It had encouraged the bacteria, and she was now just a skeleton, curled into the fetal position. She was unrecognizable, but I had no doubt in my mind it was her. And she was in possession of both her arms.

FIFTEEN

WE SPENT THE REST OF THE MORNING WITH THE sheriff. He didn't seem very amused that we'd been pursuing an investigation on his patch without his knowledge. When I explained that we were just passing through, decided to have a look at the place, and noticed the stone, he was somewhat placated, but not much.

"Passing through? You're a hundred and fifty miles off course, Detective. That may be passing through in New York, but not here. Next time you want to go digging up bodies in Dutchess County, you call me *first*. Are we clear?"

"We are clear, Sheriff."

Jurisdiction was an issue, but I was happy to let it slide, and by midday Dehan and I were in the Jag and headed back toward New York.

"Whether it's Boston PD, Connecticut, or New York, that case will end up at the bureau. I am satisfied that our arms do not belong to Lynda, and if Zak was at the rally killing Lynda, he could not have been somewhere else killing our victim—wherever she was killed. So we can, finally, eliminate Zak from our list."

"Which brings us back to Peter and Dave."

She reached in her pocket and pulled out her cell. She scrolled through her address book, selected a number, and dialed. She put it on speaker and put it on the dash. It rang a couple of times, and then a man's voice said, "Canadian American Chemicals, good afternoon, how may I help you?"

"This is Detective Dehan of the NYPD, Forty-Third Precinct. I would like to speak to Mr. Richard Chambers, head of sales."

"Speaking. How can I help you, Detective?"

"We are making some routine inquiries, sir, into an old case, and we are just tying up some loose ends and eliminating people from our investigation. I wonder if you could give me some information about an employee of yours, back in 2005."

There was a moment's silence, and then he said, "I doubt we would have records that old readily available. Who is the employee, and what do you want to know?"

"The employee is Peter Smith . . ."

"Peter?"

"We wanted to know if his work back in 2005 would have taken him to California at all?"

"Why yes, indeed. I don't need to check the files for that. Peter was instrumental in opening up the west for us, from Los Angeles down to San Diego. In 2004, 2005, and 2006 he was there for at least a week every month. He was a tireless worker, highly ambitious. He is a good friend of mine. What is this about, Detective?"

"I wonder if you could send me that information by email. I would be very grateful, Mr. Chambers." She gave him her email address, and he repeated his question. "As I said, sir, we are just tying up loose ends."

She hung up and was silent for a while, then exploded, "Son of a bitch! What were they, Stone, accomplices?"

I thought about that. It was one of the questions I had been asking myself. "I think our killer selected his venues with the same care he devoted to everything else. He chose highly populous places where there was plenty of prostitution. There is another possibility."

"What?"

"That one of them is trying to deflect suspicion onto the other."

"If that is true, only one of them was going to San Diego and Los Angeles because he had to, and that was Peter. Whereas Dave *chose* to go, and he continued going *after* the killings stopped. Plus, the arms *could* be seen as having been planted in Peter's unit. Stone, you have to admit, the evidence is just piling up against Dave."

"Yes, yes it is, Dehan. And I am not opposed to Dave as our prime suspect. I just want to be sure. As of right now, all we have is circumstantial, and I would like some real evidence. I'll tell you what we are going to do. We are going to visit Peter's wife, while Peter is out."

We got back to the station at almost three. When we got out of the car, Dehan said, "Stone, you going to see the captain about Zak?"

"Yeah, why? You want to do something else?"

"I *need* to do some shopping. It's just four or five things. I will be less than half an hour. Can I borrow your car?"

I smiled. "Of course." I threw her the key.

"Thanks, Sensei."

She climbed back in, and I watched her drive away.

I went to my desk, collected everything in the file that related to Zak, and went to see the captain. I knocked.

A big sigh and then, "Come."

He was an agreeable guy. He smiled and stood as I stepped in. He shook my hand and invited me to sit. He was in his fifties, with graying temples and an intelligent face. He was a welcome change from Jennifer.

"Stone, of Stone and Dehan. The dynamic duo. Your reputation precedes you both." He chuckled as though he'd made a joke, then asked, "What can I do for you?"

First I told him about Zak. I put the file on his desk and said, "This all has nothing to do with the cold case we're conducting, Captain. The crimes involved span at least three states. This belongs to the Feds, and I believe the sheriff of Dutchess County is contacting them himself."

He leafed through it. He had what you could only describe as a twinkle in his eye. "So you cracked this one in your spare time while you were working on mission impossible, huh?"

I was about to explain, but instead I said, "Yes, sir."

Newman chuckled. "And what about the arms? Do you think you're close to cracking that?"

"We have two suspects, but all the evidence is circumstantial at this stage." I outlined how the case stood and said, "I would really like to talk to Mrs. Smith while Peter is out. I'd like to call him to come to the station for an interview and have him wait here for half an hour while we talk to his wife. I want to rattle his cage and also see if she breaks down when he's not around."

He thought about it for a moment. "Well, it's not illegal, as long as she invites you in. And if you think it's the right way to go, I have great confidence in your abilities." He glanced at me. "I don't share Captain Cuevas' opinion of you, Stone. You may as well know that. But I am keen to see some of these cold cases resolved, and I can't think of anyone better for the job." He paused, then glanced at me again. "As you have seen in both of these cases, some of them are not quite as cold as they seem to be."

I thanked him and left, wondering if he had been hinting at something. I got back to my desk, dropped into my chair, and dialed Peter Smith's number. It rang a couple of times before he answered.

"Peter Smith speaking."

"Mr. Smith, Detective John Stone here."

A small sigh. "Detective Stone, how can I help you now?"

"Mr. Smith, our investigation is turning up quite a lot of disturbing evidence. There has been a fresh murder, and a number of notes have been received threatening further killings. We have reason to believe that you and your wife may be at risk, and we would like you to come in to the station for a talk. If possible, this afternoon."

"Both of us?"

"No, for now just you, Mr. Smith. But we will have a car keeping an eye on your house to make sure your wife is safe."

"I see . . ." He hesitated. "Very well, I can be there in an hour."

"That would be fine. We'd be very grateful. Are you at home now?"

"Yes, I work mainly from home. Why?"

"We'll have a car there before you leave."

I spoke to the desk sergeant and a couple of colleagues, and they agreed to keep him there, supplied with coffee, as long as they could. Dehan arrived, and we set out for Revere Avenue.

We parked up the road, out of sight. We watched him come out with quick, efficient steps, get into his car, and drive away. Then we got out, walked across the wet blacktop, and climbed the steps to the Smiths' door. Jenny opened the door and looked surprised.

"Oh! He's just gone . . ."

I smiled. "We'll catch up with him. There were just a couple of questions we wanted to ask you, in fact. May we come in?"

She hesitated, and Dehan jumped up and down with knock-knees and grinning. "Can I use your toilet? It's this rain!"

Jenny got flustered and said, "Yes! Yes of course, come in!"

And we were in.

While Dehan skipped up the stairs to the bathroom, I smiled at Jenny in what I hoped was a fatherly way.

"We are very concerned for your safety, Jenny. And it is extremely important for us to make sure that both you and Peter are eliminated from any suspicion . . ."

"Suspicion? *Us?*"

I sighed and shrugged. "There are some very unscrupulous defense attorneys out there who will do anything to get their clients off. So I hope you will cooperate fully with us in preempting any ploys they may try."

She looked suitably horrified and said, "Why, yes! Of course! How can I help?"

I thought about it a moment and asked, "What kind of shoes does your husband wear?"

"*Shoes?*" She gave a small laugh. "Well, as you ask, he has rather particular taste. He always says that however badly dressed a man is, you can always tell a gentleman by his shoes."

"How very true."

"So he has his shoes made especially for him in Spain, of all places. I tell him we have very good shoemakers here in the States. But he gets cross. These, he says, are the best, handmade from Spanish leather. So that's what he wears."

"I imagine he buys them online. What is the name of the company?"

"Yes, that's right. Gallardo. But what has this to do . . . ?"

"Nothing," I lied. "I just happened to notice the other day what excellent shoes he had, and thought I'd ask. But surely he doesn't wear them in this terrible weather?"

"Oh, they are quite waterproof!"

"Would you think me an awful bore if I asked to see them? I am thinking of buying some good shoes myself, and . . ."

You could tell she was uncomfortable, but she had lived her entire life without ever learning to say no, and she wasn't about to start now. So she rose and went upstairs, and I, quite shamelessly, followed her into their bedroom.

She stood in the middle of the floor saying, "I really don't think . . ." But as she said it, Dehan stepped in from the toilet and I pointed to the wardrobe. "Are they in there?"

"Yes, but . . ."

"Thank you, Jenny. We'll leave it just as it was."

There were three pairs of Oxford brogues. They were all clean. I hunkered down and examined them. The tread pattern fit. I put them all back as I had found them. I asked her, "Are any of these the ones he was wearing five nights ago?"

She stammered. "He rotates them, a new pair every day, from left to right."

I did a quick calculation and decided he would have been

wearing the ones on the far left. I picked them up and smelled the soles. Then I put them back.

I stood and closed the wardrobe. "Are you a heavy sleeper, Mrs. Smith?"

"No, I sleep very badly. That's why Peter insists that I take a tablet every night."

"So six nights ago, if Peter had got up during the night, you would not have noticed?"

"No, but why on Earth would he have got up?"

"Thank you, Mrs. Smith. You have been very helpful. We had better get after Peter, or we'll miss him."

SIXTEEN

She watched us leave, with her hands clenched in front of her womb. The sky was turning black, and thunder rolled far off. A few fat drops fell as we climbed into the Jag and pulled away, and Dehan swore extensively in three languages. I paid no attention because my brain was busy putting all the pieces together.

Finally she looked at me as though she was going to hit me. "Have you *any* idea what is going on? Does this make *any* sense to you *at all*? Are they? Are they accomplices? Are they in this together?"

I was still ignoring her, but I said, "I'll get another note this evening or tonight. Probably this evening. It will probably come to the station. It will probably have a date for the next killing, or something close."

"How . . . how can you possibly know that?"

I glanced at her. "Wait. I'm thinking."

I pulled up outside the precinct and ran up the stairs. Frank, who'd been keeping Peter happy for me, grabbed my arm. "He's in interrogation room three, and he's pissed."

"Thanks."

I pushed into the room with Dehan on my tail. Peter looked

up. His eyes were bright with indignation. "Do you know how long . . . ?"

I cut across him. "How long have you been wearing Spanish shoes?"

"*What?*"

"*How long,* Peter?"

"I don't know . . ." He screwed up his face at me. I waited. "Since I was . . . About fifteen years. What in the name of heaven . . . ?"

I closed the door. Dehan was looking at me like I was crazy. They both were. I pulled up a chair and sat down.

"I haven't got time to fuck around, Peter. So forgive me if I am blunt. You are not a very nice person. There must be a few people at work who really don't like you. I need to know who they are."

"How dare you . . . !"

"Deal with it! Now tell me! *Who?*"

He went to stand. "I don't have to . . ."

"*Who?*"

He looked flustered and a little scared. "Um . . . Johnson, Cohen, Brown . . ."

"Any others?"

"Not really . . ."

"Did *any* of them travel to California with you in 2005?"

He frowned. "No. I went alone."

I was quiet for a while, thinking. I walked to the door, opened it, and bellowed, "Any messages for me?" A few blank faces looked and shook their heads. I closed the door and looked at Peter. "You know David?"

"David? What David? I know a couple of Davids."

"From the Global Computer Shipping Company. They own the units . . ."

"Yes. We've exchanged the odd nod. He's supplied me with my computers over the years. Odd fellow, but helpful."

"Over the years?"

He shrugged and shook his head. "Ten, maybe more . . . fifteen."

"Ever run across him in San Diego?"

"No . . ."

"L.A.?"

"*No . . . !*"

"You realize we can check, and if we find you're lying, that will count against you."

"In what? For God's sake, Detective! What in the name of God is going on here?"

"Let me see your shoes." He stared at me, and his face flushed. He looked as though he was about to get violent. I said, "Are you refusing to show me your shoes?"

He took a deep breath. "I am going to show you my shoes. Then I am going to go home. If you want to keep me, then charge me with something, but it had better be something more than wearing Spanish shoes or knowing David. Frankly, Detective, your behavior is bordering on the irrational."

"Your shoes."

He unlaced them, took them off, and slammed them on the table. I looked at them carefully and smelled the soles. I handed them back to him.

"Thank you, Mr. Smith. I apologize for the inconvenience. You can go."

He stared at me in disgust. "You people. No wonder this country is going to the dogs!"

He put his shoes back on, and as he slammed out, a uniform leaned in. "Note delivered for you . . ."

I pushed past her and ran. I took the stairs a landing at a time and shouted at the desk sergeant, "*Who delivered the note?*"

He pointed at the door. "Kid—he just left, in a hoodie . . ."

I leapt out of the door into the gathering night as Dehan came clattering after me. It was raining. There was a young man, maybe a hundred yards away, hunched in a dark hoodie, passing through a pool of misty light cast by a streetlamp. I heard the sergeant shout, "That's him!"

Dehan and I took off at a sprint down the wet road. The guy must have heard us coming because he looked back and started to run. We caught him at the corner and slammed him against the wall of the deli.

"I ain't done nothin'! I ain't done nothin', man! Let me go!"

Dehan snarled, "You ain't done nothing? Why'd you run?"

"You was chasin' me! I ran!"

Dehan cuffed him, and I turned him around. He was about eighteen, black, and scared.

"Tell me about the note."

He shrugged and glanced from me to Dehan and back again, wondering which one of us to be scared of. "I don't know nothin' about the note. Guy said to deliver it to the desk sergeant. That's what I done. I never even read it."

I wiped water from my eyes. "What's this guy look like?"

"Average height. Jeans, dark hoodie. Big shades and a scarf around his mouth. He give me fifty bucks and said he'd be watchin'. If I didn't deliver it, bad things was gonna happen."

I sighed. "Okay, come on. You're going to make a statement. Then you can go home. Uncuff him, Dehan."

I left the kid in the hands of a sergeant who took his statement, and Dehan and I went back to have a look at the note. It was still sitting on the table in the interrogation room. It was a piece of A4 photographic paper, folded in half. On the outside it simply bore my name, but on the inside, taking up half the page, there was a photograph. It looked like a photo of a shopping mall at dusk taken from the parking lot. There was a brightly lit door and a woman walking in through that door, toward the shops. In the foreground there were several cars out of focus. There was a time and date stamp on the photograph. It had been taken two hours earlier, while I was on the phone to Peter. On the top half, above the photograph, there was printed, "Tick tock, tick tock . . ."

"Where is this place? Who is this woman?"

Dehan was thinking fast. "It has to be within two hours' drive in rush-hour traffic."

"That could be thirty, forty square miles or more." I yanked open the door and hollered, "*Somebody! Anybody! Now!*"

A sergeant came running, looking alarmed. "I need a list, ten minutes ago, of all the major malls in the Bronx, with photographs."

She could have told me to go to hell and do it myself, but she didn't. She said, "I can do that for you."

"No, wait!" I turned to Dehan. "The Bronx is what, seven miles across at its widest. Ten miles long, I am being approximate here. It's rush hour. He has to select his victim, photograph her, get to a printer, write his message, print the photograph, and then deliver it. For that, he needs to select a suitable messenger who is willing to deliver. All of this is eating considerably into his two hours. So we need malls that are close to the precinct."

The sergeant said, "Yes, we have Bruckner Plaza, New Horizons, Webster . . ."

"Photographs!" I showed her the picture. "Find this mall. Because that woman is going to be killed."

"I'm on it."

I ran up the stairs to the captain. I knocked and went in without waiting. He looked up, startled. I showed him the picture. "I need a BOLO on this woman. I need cars to go to every mall in the Bronx and identify this shopping center—and this woman. They need to talk to cashiers, shop assistants. The clock is ticking on this woman's life."

He nodded. "Yes. I'll see to it."

He was picking up the phone as I left.

When I got back down, the sergeant was talking to Dehan. She looked at me as I approached. "Maria thinks it's the New Horizons. I think so too. I was just there."

"I'm pretty sure it is, Detective."

"Okay, thanks, Maria. Dehan, get your coat. Let's go."

As we ran down to the car, she said, "Why don't we just go get Dave?"

"Because if it's him, we'll waste time looking for him and we won't find him. And if it's not him, we'll find him, but it will be a waste of time."

"Oh . . ."

It took us ten minutes to get there, and another fifteen to run around the parking lot checking every entrance to see if it fit. Then Dehan grabbed my arm and stopped me. "Look."

I looked at the photograph, then at the building, at the door, the tree, the letters . . . I shook my head. "No, the tree is in the wrong place."

"No! It's not. Look at the letters on the wall, up in the corner. You can hardly see them, but look carefully."

I frowned. "They should be over there . . ."

"Look again, Stone!"

"They're back to front! Son of a bitch! He's inverted the picture!"

"It's this mall, this entrance."

We ran in. Over on the right there was a Pathmark. I pointed at the nearest checkout. "You start there. I'll start at the other end."

There was a long line, but I barged in waving my badge.

"Excuse the interruption, folks," I said to the guy at the checkout. "Were you here two hours ago?"

"Sure. Been here since one."

"Do you recognize this woman? Her life might be at risk."

He looked blank and shook his head. I showed it around to the people in the line and got the same blank response. I moved to the next checkout. Same thing. Third one I was getting the same blank stares and shaking heads when I heard my name being called. It was Dehan, waving to me. She was six checkouts down. I ran to her. As I approached, she was saying, "This woman knows her."

The woman at the checkout was large and in her fifties. She

looked worried. "She comes in three or four times a week. She's a nice lady. She lives two streets from me on the corner. She in trouble?" The people in line were not sure whether to be restless or curious. There was some sighing and muttering.

I shook my head. "No, but she could be at risk. We need to find her. It's really urgent. Where does she live?"

"I'll write it down for you, honey."

While she was writing it down, a big guy in a vest and a baseball cap started complaining. "Hey, we all got problems. Move it along. The woman's got a fuckin' problem, take it somewhere else. This is a goddamn store."

Dehan turned to him. "Hey! Mister. You got an attitude?"

"I ain't got an attitude, I just wanna do my fuckin' shopping."

"I'm asking you if you've got a fucking attitude! I got a fucking attitude, see? I got a bad fucking attitude. If you ain't got a bad fucking attitude like mine, then shut the fuck up. We clear?"

I glanced at him. He had gone the color and consistency of a suet dumpling. I thanked the woman at the checkout, and we left at a run. We ran through the dark, wet parking lot, and as we scrambled into the car, I grabbed the radio.

"Detectives Stone and Dehan requesting backup at 1820B Waterloo Place. Have located woman in APB. Heading there now from New Horizons Shopping Mall."

I hit the gas, and as I pulled out of the lot, I glanced at Dehan and said, "You have got a *fucking* attitude, Dehan."

"I have a fucking attitude. You ain't got a fucking attitude? Have you got a fucking attitude, Stone?"

"I've got a fucking attitude. Have you got a fucking attitude?"

"I've got a fucking attitude."

It was less than a two-minute drive. Waterloo Place was a short, quiet street with a mixture of apartment blocks and well-kept houses with gabled roofs and ample porches. I came to 1820B and screeched to a halt. As we made our way onto the porch, I could hear sirens approaching. There was light in the windows, but I couldn't hear any sounds coming from inside. I pressed the bell.

Nothing.

I pressed the bell and hammered on the door. A squad car came wailing into the street and stopped outside the house. I hammered again. Car doors slammed, and the two patrolmen were running up to join us.

A door slammed inside the house. Then there were running feet clattering down the stairs. I stood back and pulled my piece. Dehan did the same. The patrolmen covered us.

The door was wrenched open and a woman stood there, a look of absolute horror on her face, her hair disheveled and a bath towel wrapped around her. She stared at us and said, "What the *hell* is going on?"

SEVENTEEN

HER NAME WAS NANCY PIERCE. WE SAT WITH HER IN her living room. She had put a bathrobe on and now had a towel wound around her head. Dehan was sitting next to her, and I was opposite. The patrol car was outside awaiting instructions. Nancy Pierce looked like she had just discovered that for the past thirty years she'd been living on the Truman Show. Everything had changed and nothing would ever be quite the same again.

She kept asking, "*Why . . . ?*"

I kept wanting to tell her that wasn't a helpful question, but I knew that wouldn't have been a helpful answer either. Finally, Dehan said to her, "Nancy, you have to stop asking yourself that. The whole point is that there is no motive. He is crazy. If you try to understand him, you'll drive yourself crazy too."

Nancy looked at Dehan as though she was crazy. I asked her, "Have you got anybody you can stay with?"

She stared at me a moment, then said, "*No . . .*" like now I was crazy too. "I mean, I have a sister, but she has kids . . . How could I . . . ?"

She couldn't finish the sentence. I nodded that I understood. "We'll leave a patrol car outside. You want a policewoman to stay here tonight?" She nodded. "Okay, we'll arrange that."

I made the call, and while Dehan sat with Nancy, I went around the house, checking the windows and the access points to see if there was any way he could get in. By the time I was finished, I was satisfied that, unless he was Spider-Man, the only way in for him was past the patrol car and the policewoman who was going to be sitting downstairs with her service .38, watching TV all night.

Sergeant Maria Fernadez, who had identified the shopping mall back at the station, volunteered and turned up within about fifteen minutes. When she and Nancy had settled in, I stepped outside into the drizzle with Dehan. I studied her face a moment. She looked exhausted.

"Stone, pull David in before he kills somebody."

"The smallest miscalculation now and we could blow the whole thing, and that could cost many more lives, Dehan."

"He is going to kill, just to show you he can."

"On what grounds do we arrest him? And on what grounds do we hold him?" She looked away from me. Her jaw muscle was bouncing. "The closest thing we have to actual evidence points to Peter, not to Dave."

She sighed and rubbed her face. "I know. What do you want me to do?"

"Go home. I want you to go home, disconnect, and rest. I'll call you in the morning."

"What about you?"

"I'm okay for the moment. I've got a couple of things I want to look into. Then I'll get some sleep too."

"Okay." She sighed. "But anything, and I mean *anything*, you call me. You understand?"

I smiled at her. "Don't worry about it. Come on, I'll drop you off."

It was a short drive, and we made it in silence, with only the slow, steady squeak of the windshield wipers and the wet hiss of the traffic outside. Inside the cocoon of the cab, the silence was almost comforting. Almost safe.

I pulled up in front of the big red stone building, and we sat a moment looking at each other.

"Call me, okay?"

I smiled. "I'm never sure how long to leave it. Two days seems a long time, but a day can seem needy."

"Dork."

"Hey, that was my nickname at school."

"Good night, Stone."

"Good night, Dehan."

I watched her climb the five steps and let herself in. The door closed behind her, and I sat for five minutes wondering what to do.

I drove first to Revere Avenue and cruised slowly past the Smiths' house. Then I drove up past Dave's house. I didn't know what I expected to see, but whatever it was, I didn't see it. Then I drove back to Nancy Pierce's house and parked. I was about to get out and ask the patrolmen if there was anything to report when my phone rang. The number was withheld. I answered.

"Stone."

There was a stifled giggle.

"Who is this?"

Then a voice that was mainly breath said, "*Tick . . . tock . . . tick . . . tock . . .*"

There was a moment's silence, and the line went dead.

I called the precinct and told them to trace the last call to my number, but I knew it would be a disposable cell.

I got out and walked to the squad car. There was a hollow crunch to my steps. The wet road looked like polished bronze. The street was empty and cold. I leaned on the car. The patrolman had the window open and was looking up at me.

"Jones, right?"

"Yes, Detective."

"He just called me. Stay alert. He could be nearby."

He nodded.

I walked around the side of the house and into the back

garden. It was very dark. The fence and the shed at the end were blacker shapes against the blackness. I took my time exploring every corner. The shed was locked. The garden was empty, and there was nobody on the other side of the fences. I went back around to the front and rang the bell. The sergeant opened up and let me in. I could hear the TV in the next room. I spoke quietly.

"He called."

"What did he say?"

I shook my head. "Tick tock."

"You think he's here?"

"I don't know. Is she asleep?"

She shook her head.

We went through to the living room. Nancy looked up, questioning me with her eyes. I smiled, though it wasn't from the heart. "Everything is quiet."

"What about tomorrow?"

"We are going to catch him."

I sat on the sofa and pulled out the photograph of the mall. There was something about it that was wrong. I couldn't put my finger on what it was, but there was something nagging at the back of my mind. Dehan had been smart to see how it had been inverted, the relationship of the tree to the door and the letters. Nine out of ten people would not have spotted it, especially in a rush. That told me this guy was cunning.

The way he had angled and focused the shot so that any identifying marks were outside the frame. All you could really see was the big double glass doors with the light pouring out from inside. Then there was Nancy right in the middle of the doorway, reaching out with what seemed to be her right hand but was really her left. That made sense because she was holding something, a bag, with her right hand.

"You're right-handed?"

She glanced at me. "Yeah . . ."

And then everything in the foreground was dark and out of

focus. It was as though there was a split, two distinct parts to the picture. The dark blur of the foreground, and the bright clarity of the background.

I felt the hair on my head prickle, and I went cold. I was suddenly aware that I had been extremely stupid. I still wasn't sure why, or how, but something in my mind was screaming at me that if the background was clear and the foreground was dark and blurry, the foreground was where I needed to be looking.

This was not about Nancy Pierce.

Then things started to slot into place. The hazy, grainy figure getting into or out of the car right in the foreground was wrong. It was what had been troubling me since Dehan spotted that the photograph was inverted. Because the person getting in or out was on the *left* of the car. You could just make out the steering wheel. But if the picture was inverted it ought to be on the other side.

My brain was scrambling. Had he cut the picture in half and only inverted the top? That didn't make any sense. What would be the point of doing that? So what other explanation could there be? The only explanation was that the car wasn't American. The car was English.

"*Shit!*" I shouted and ran. "Maria! Call Dehan. Tell her to be armed and check her apartment. He's going after her! I'm on my way!"

I scrambled into my car and hit the gas. I called for backup and burned rubber down Crotona Park North, did sixty the wrong way on Crotona Park East, and skidded onto Southern Boulevard. Then I floored the pedal. It took me less than a minute to cover the mile, and it was a miracle I didn't kill myself or somebody else. I screamed right into 167th, floored the pedal again, and then screamed left at the junction, going the wrong way again, into Dehan's street. I skidded to a halt outside her door and jumped out.

My phone was ringing. It was Maria. "She's not answering."

I could hear sirens approaching.

"Okay. I'm here."

I hung up and pressed all the bells at the same time. As they answered, I yelled, "NYPD! Open up!"

The lock buzzed. I slammed through and ran up the stairs. She was on the fifth. By the time I got there I was gasping for air and my legs were shaking, but I didn't pause. I pulled my piece, shot out the lock, and pushed in, screaming, *"Dehan! Dehan!"*

I checked the kitchen. It was clear. I burst into the living room. The light was on, but the room was empty. I was still screaming her name like a maniac. It was a one-bedroom apartment. I could only have been there a few seconds. I kicked in the bedroom door, holding my gun out in front of me.

The bedroom was dark, but the bathroom door was open and there was light coming out. There was a figure in the bathroom door, in silhouette, staring at me. It took me a full three seconds to register that it was Dehan. She was wearing pajamas, and her hair was wet. "What the fuck, Stone . . . ?"

I was aware that I was shaking. I tried to control it and said, "You're okay . . ." It wasn't a question.

"Yeah. I'm okay . . ."

I went to her and put my arms around her, hugging her hard for a couple of seconds, more to reassure myself that she was okay. I let her go and looked into her face. She was smiling uncertainly. I heard voices calling from the door.

"Detective Stone! NYPD!"

"Okay, I'm here." I holstered my piece and stepped out. "Sorry, guys, another false alarm."

The patrolman pointed at the blown lock. "What's this?"

"I thought Detective Dehan was at risk."

He frowned curiously at me. "You got this?"

"I've got it."

"Okay . . ."

They left and I went back to Dehan. She was standing in her bedroom door.

"You want to tell me what's going on?"

"You weren't answering your phone."

"I was in the shower. I guess I didn't hear it. But that's no reason to shoot out my lock, Stone."

"Sit down."

She sat on the sofa, and I sat next to her. I showed her the photograph. "Look at the car in the foreground. Look at the woman who's about to open the door."

She stared at it a moment, frowning. Then she gave an involuntary intake of breath, and her hand went to her mouth. She stared at me, and she looked scared.

"Dehan, it was never about Nancy. He called me after I dropped you off. He was laughing. All he said was, 'tick tock.' It made me look at the photograph again. He must have taken it when you borrowed my car to go shopping."

"I'm his fucking target? I'm not even blond!"

"Pack a bag. You're coming back to my place, and I am going to stick to you like glue."

She nodded, and for a moment she looked small and vulnerable. "Thanks, Stone."

EIGHTEEN

I PUT HER TO BED IN THE SPARE ROOM, AND I SAT IN THE living room watching TV till the sky turned gray over a wet dawn. Then I climbed the stairs and looked in on her. She was sleeping, snoring softly. I sat in the armchair in the corner and closed my eyes. That must have been about six thirty.

It felt like I had just closed my eyes, but I felt her shaking me gently, and when I opened them, she was showered and dressed, and there was a gray light in the room. I looked at the bedside clock. It was seven thirty.

She said, "Get in the bed, Stone. Get a couple of hours' sleep. I'll call you at nine thirty for breakfast."

I shook my head. "Make bacon and coffee. I'll be down in twenty. I'll get some sleep this afternoon."

I had a cold shower, which got rid of the grogginess, and then the smell of bacon and coffee did the rest. I sat, and she piled my plate with rashers, two eggs, and toast. Then she poured my coffee and sat opposite me.

"Stone, we have to pull Dave in."

I ate, drank coffee, and thought.

"Okay." I ate, drank, and thought a bit more. "On what charge?"

"Not arrest him. Interrogate him. Put him under pressure and see what happens to him."

I looked at her and nodded. "Yeah. Okay."

DAVID WAS at his office and agreed to come with us without any objection. Fischer came out to see what was going on and took me aside.

"Are you arresting him?"

"No, we just want to ask him some questions down at the station."

"Does he need a lawyer?"

"That's up to him, Mr. Fischer, but we are not accusing him of anything."

He looked past me at where David was standing with Dehan, staring at his feet. "David, do you want me to call Sam?"

David didn't say anything. He just shook his head.

We drove in silence. Dehan sat by his side in the back and stared at him all the way. Even in the mirror I could tell he was nervous. We put him in the interrogation room and asked him if he wanted coffee. He said he didn't. I took Dehan outside the room and asked her, "You want to sit this one out?"

She shook her head. "No."

"Okay. But I want you cool."

She said she was cool, and we went back in. We sat. He was sitting with his feet together and his hands in his lap. His eyes were lowered.

I took a moment to think, then said, "David, I was just wondering if you could clarify a few things for me that I don't understand."

His jaw was rigid when he answered, like he was trying to talk with his mouth closed.

"If I can . . ."

"You told your uncle that twice a year, in July and December, you attend computer conventions and conferences so that you can stay abreast of developments in the IT world."

His eyes shifted around, left and right, like he was mentally measuring the tabletop. I waited, and after a while he said, "That's not a question. I don't know how to answer you."

Dehan looked at me like she wanted to slap him around the head. I ignored her.

"Okay, that's true. Is it also true that you told your uncle that you attend those IT conferences?"

His cheeks colored and he gave a very small, private smile.

"Yes."

"Now, here's the thing. We checked and we found that there are no fixed IT conferences for those dates, every year. So, what I would like to know is, what have you been doing for the last twelve years, when your uncle thought you were attending IT conferences?"

He was silent again, with his eyes darting this way and that and his jaw working. Dehan said, "You going to answer the question, David?"

I glanced at her, but she ignored me.

I sighed. "I know it's a difficult question to answer, Dave . . ."

"David."

"David. I know it's a difficult question to answer . . ."

"I have to insist on being called David."

I paused. Dehan sighed.

I asked him, "Is that a decision you made for yourself, David?"

"Yes."

"Did somebody help you to make that decision?"

"Yes."

"Who helped you?"

"Dr. Stephens."

"Is Dr. Stephens your psychologist?"

"Psychiatrist."

"How long have you been seeing Dr. Stephens?"

"Thirteen years, th-three months, and four days."

I gave a small laugh of admiration. "You have quite a memory."

He smiled, and there was clearly pleasure in his face. "I have an ei-eidetic memory. I have almost t-total recall."

He was stammering on his longer sentences.

"I know a few psychiatrists. They are interesting people. They don't see things the same way as other people, do they?"

He shook his head and murmured, "They're smart."

"They're smart," I agreed. "Like, most people would think telling the truth is good, lying is bad, right?"

His eyes were darting again, and his jaw started working. This was his tell, but it was a tell that said he was trying to frame a sentence.

"Dr.-Dr. Stephens says, do w-what you need to do . . . t-to get strong . . ."

Dehan snapped, "Does that include killing young women?"

His face went crimson, and his eyes locked on to the table like a vice. I glared at Dehan. Her cheeks were flushed, and her eyes were bright with anger.

"Will you excuse us a moment, David? Detective Dehan, a word outside, please." We stepped into the corridor. I closed the door and said, "Are you going to hold it together or not? You just sabotaged my interrogation. I'm going to try and get it back on track, but I don't know how much damage you've done."

"I'm sorry. I'll keep it together."

"He's not going to talk with you in the room. For now just stay in the observation room."

She nodded. "Okay. I'm sorry."

I went back in and sat down. "Wooh! Women!"

He smiled, but he looked scared.

"You never know what they are going to do next. So, where were we? We were talking about Dr. Stephens. And if I under-stand you, he advised you to lie to your uncle and your mother about where you go in July and December. Am I right?" Before he could answer, I went on. "I want you to know that as far as I can see, I don't need to tell your uncle and your mother that you have been lying to them."

I gave him a while to think about that.

"So did he advise you to lie to them?"

He nodded. "Yes."

"Okay, a good doctor. So let's start with the cities you go to. Where do you go in July?"

He stared hard into the right-hand corner of the room. This was a different tell. Now he was deciding if he wanted to tell me or not. Finally, he said, "San Diego."

"Nice town. How about December?"

"L-Los Angeles."

"L.A., huh? Okay, David, we are doing really well." He smiled. "Now what I need to understand is what it is you do in San Diego in July."

His face flushed and his eyes shone. He stared hard into the corner. I raised my hands and gave a small laugh. "Hey! I'm with Dr. Stephens. Whatever it takes to get you strong."

He licked his lips, kept pursing them. There were tears in his eyes. "B-bring your . . . bring your dreams a-a . . ."

"Alive?"

He nodded. He looked like he thought I was going to start beating him. I thought for a while. After a bit, I said, "That's all any of us want. There is nothing wrong with that, is there?"

He shook his head. "Mom . . . Mom and Uncle Howard say that m-my dreams are ch-ch . . ."

"Childish?"

"Yes. And w-w . . ."

"Wicked?"

"Yes."

"What is it about your dreams that they say is childish and wicked? Can you give me an example?"

"B-B . . ." He paused. "Batman. Conan . . ."

"You like Marvel and DC comics, huh? I like them myself. I once met Stan 'the Man' Lee in person."

He was smiling into the corner. "I shook his hand."

"So are you telling me you go to Comic-Con?"

"Yes."

"And how about in the evenings?" The smile faded. "Did Dr. Stephens tell you not to talk about it?" He nodded. "But you can tell me, David. Just like you told me everything else, because you know I get it. I understand."

His face flushed again, and he stared down at his fingers. He was ashamed—ashamed of his pleasure. "I visit my f-friends."

"Girlfriends?"

He nodded.

"Do you enjoy those visits?"

Again the secret smile. "Th-they do nice things to me . . ."

"Does Dr. Stephens give you special pills to help with that?"

"I h-had e-e . . ." He stopped and breathed. "Erectile d-dysf-f . . ."

"Dysfunction? You had erectile dysfunction?"

"But he gave me pills. Now I'm okay . . ."

I nodded. "That's good. Let me see your shoes, David, will you?"

He frowned at me. He pulled his chair back and stood up, then walked around so I could look down at his shoes. They were blue-and-white Converse trainers.

"Thanks. They're nice shoes. Do you have any special leather shoes that you use for special occasions?"

He shook his head. "No. These are the only sh-shoes I like."

"Okay, David, let's take a break. I'm going to take you back to work in a while. But for now just take a break. You okay?"

He nodded at the corner.

I stepped outside and opened the door to the observation room. It was empty. I poked my head into the detectives' room. She wasn't at our desk. I asked a couple of people. Nobody had seen her. I went downstairs. I looked outside. It was raining. Don was on the desk. "You seen Detective Dehan?"

"Yeah. She went out about five minutes ago."

I called her on my cell. It rang a couple of times, then cut off. I looked at my watch. Maybe she was at the deli getting lunch. My phone rang. It was Dehan. I felt an unexpected surge of relief. I pressed the green button and said, "Where are you?"

There was a moment's silence, and then a giggle and a voice that was almost all breath said, "*Tick . . . tock . . . tick . . . tock . . .*"

NINETEEN

I HAD A STRANGE SENSATION LIKE THE WORLD ROCKED. I could hear the blood pounding in my head, and there was a voice telling me it was essential to stay calm and focused because Dehan's life depended on me not fucking up. My hands were shaking, but I managed to call Bernie at the bureau.

"Bernie, he has Dehan . . ."

"What are you talking about, Stone?"

"I haven't got time to explain. He took her in the last five or ten minutes."

"Who did? You're not making sense."

"The serial killer! The guy who cut off the girl's arms twelve years ago, goddamn it! He took Dehan about five minutes ago. I need you to trace her GPS on her phone!"

"You've got techs who can do that . . ."

"For crying out loud, Bernie! By the time I get through the red tape she could be dead! *Just do it!*"

I was shouting. Several people turned to look at me.

"Okay, buddy. Take it easy. I'll do it."

I went inside and ran up the stairs to the captain. I went in without knocking.

"Stone!"

"Dehan has been abducted."

"*What?* When? By whom?"

"The serial killer we've been tracking down. She was convinced it was David Hansen. But while I was interrogating him, she was abducted." I told him about the phone call.

He was reaching for the phone. "We can have them track her GPS."

"The bureau are on it already."

He looked startled.

"It was quicker. We need a BOLO."

He frowned. "But what are we looking out for?"

"*I don't know! Goddamn it!*"

"Get a grip, Stone. She needs you cool right now."

I breathed. "Put out a BOLO on Detective Dehan. Approach with extreme care. She has been abducted. Also, an all points, I need to talk to the last person who saw Detective Dehan when she left the building. There must have been patrolmen or women coming in and out."

As I was talking, I was leaving his office and running down the stairs. I went to the desk sergeant and took him aside.

"Don. Dehan has been abducted."

"Shit!"

"You saw her step outside. I need to talk to any patrolmen and women who were coming in or leaving and may have seen her."

He nodded. "Yeah! Andersen was going out just behind her. She's outside now. She ain't left yet . . ."

I was already running, shouting, "Andersen! *Andersen!*"

She was just climbing in her car. She stopped and turned to face me.

"Hey, Detective . . ."

"You saw Dehan, ten, fifteen minutes ago."

"Sure."

"She was abducted moments after you saw her."

"Holy . . ."

"Think. Where was she going? What was she doing? What vehicles were near her . . . ?"

She stared at me.

"Let's go inside. I need a full statement from you. Every second is crucial."

As we were going in, my phone rang. It was Bernie.

"Stone!"

"We've located her phone."

"*Where?*"

"Headed north on I-95. Our techs are talking to your techs, and there's an agent talking to your captain right now."

I said to Andersen, "Talk to the captain!" I ran for my car. "Bernie, I am in pursuit. What channel do I need?"

He told me. I fired up the Jag and took off toward the I-95 like a bat out of hell. I tuned the radio as I went and checked in.

"Detective John Stone, headed east on the Bruckner Expressway in pursuit of suspect vehicle headed north on I-95."

The voice came back over the radio.

"We have an eye in the sky, Detective. What is your vehicle?"

"A 1964 Jaguar Mark II, burgundy, doing one hundred miles per hour."

The radio crackled. "I see you, Detective. Suspect vehicle is about two miles ahead of you doing fifty miles per hour. You should be on him in a little less than two minutes, Detective."

I was weaving in and out of the traffic trying to keep the needle at 100. I was pissing a lot of people off, but I didn't give a damn.

"Describe the suspect vehicle? What am I looking for?"

"Dark seven-seater, smoked windows. Could be a Chrysler."

A big SUV pulled out in front of me. I braked, swerved, almost hit a truck, switched lanes, and hit the gas. I watched the needle climb to one twenty, which was about as fast as she'd go.

The radio crackled again.

"You are approaching your target, Detective. He's about a quarter of a mile ahead of you, and you are closing fast. He is in the slow lane just going under the Country Club Road bridge now. He's about eighteen or twenty cars ahead of you."

I kept going, swerving, weaving, jumping lanes. I switched the channel and barked, "Dispatch! Where is my backup?"

More hiss and crackle and, "We have four cars about to intercept at Pelham Bay Park."

I switched channels again and started to slow.

Crackle. "He is ten cars ahead of you on your right. Nine cars . . . eight . . . seven . . . You should have visual now, Detective. Dark Chrysler, seven-seater, smoked windows . . ."

"I see him."

I pulled into the next lane and eased up behind him. I figured if he looked, he'd catch sight of me in his mirror, and that suited me fine. I wanted this son of a bitch to panic. He could see me, but he couldn't see the four patrol cars that were about to descend on him and box him in.

They came in behind us as we passed the junction. The guy didn't accelerate. He maintained his fifty miles per hour and stayed in the slow lane. Two of the patrol cars pulled ahead and slipped in, one in front of him and the other in front of me. Meanwhile, behind us, the other two cars did the same. He didn't try to squeeze out or ram us. He didn't panic.

The other drivers on the road could see something was going down and were giving us a wide berth. The squad cars had their lights flashing now, and the car behind blasted his siren and hailed him.

"*Pull over to the side of the road! Kill your engine. Put your hands out of the window and remain in your car.*"

The Chrysler indicated right and began to slow, then pulled onto the hard shoulder and stopped. The uniforms were climbing out of their cars and drawing their weapons. I didn't wait. I didn't give a damn about procedure. I jumped out and ran. He was opening the window to show us his hands. I wrenched open the door and dragged him out.

He was about five eleven, two hundred and twenty pounds,

dark and swarthy. I had never seen him before in my life. I slammed him against the side of the van. Patrolmen were running up, pulling open the other doors, shouting, "*Clear! Clear!*"

I didn't bother cuffing him. Right then what I most wanted in the world was for him to take a swing at me. My face was an inch from his, and I snarled, "Where is she, you son of a bitch? *Where is she?*"

He looked terrified.

"Who?"

They had every door on the vehicle open. They were searching the floor, under the seats, and in the glove compartments. There was nothing.

I lowered my voice so only he could hear me. "I swear to you, if you have harmed a hair, if you have hurt her in any way . . . Tell me where she is, or I will not answer for what I do next . . ."

There was an icy wind coming in off the river, but he was sweating, and I could feel his legs trembling. "Look, I am on my way to pick up my family because we're going away for the weekend. I have no idea who you're looking for, or why you think I have her. You've made some kind of mistake . . ."

Even through my rage, I could see something was wrong. I asked him, "Where have you come from?"

"I . . . um . . ."

"*Where were you before you drove here?*"

"The pharmacy . . ."

"Rite Aid? On Storey and Croes?"

"Yeah . . ."

"*Shit!*"

Right at the back of the station, with a large parking lot. She had been there—*right there!*—in the lot, while I was on the phone to Bernie, talking to the captain. I got on the ground, lay on my back, and crawled under the van. It took me two minutes to find it. It was stuck with duct tape to the bottom of the chassis, by the side door.

I scrambled out, stood up, and looked at it. My heart was

pounding. I wasn't close to panic. I was panicking. The screen displayed a timer. It was set to go off in three hours. I peeled off the tape and put it in an evidence bag. I gave it to one of the patrolmen. "Take this to the lab. It is absolute priority. Detective Dehan has three hours, then she dies. You understand me? See if they can get any prints off it. Do it now."

They ran and the car took off with sirens wailing. I returned to the driver. I showed him my badge and told him my name. "I need you to think real hard. Did you see anything—*anything*—that struck you as odd or out of place near your vehicle? Anyone standing nearby?"

He shook his head.

"Who was parked next to you?"

"I don't know, Detective. They were cars, just normal cars. There was nothing out of the ordinary." He hesitated. "About . . ." He closed his eyes, counting in his mind, his right hand held out, positioning to the vehicle in his mind. "Four cars down, opposite, an old, beat-up Cherokee Jeep. Dark green. It stood out because it was old. Maybe early nineties. But that is all."

My cell rang. It was the captain.

I said to the guy, "Listen. I'm sorry. Give your details to the sergeant. We may need to talk to you again." I walked back to my car, answering the phone. "He is playing us like a fucking violin. He had Dehan's phone taped to the underside of this guy's chassis . . ."

"Stone, listen to me."

"What?"

"It's Zak."

"What about him?" Before he could answer, I went on, "Captain, when I recovered the phone, it was set on a timer. It's set for three hours. We all know what that means. He is going to kill her in three hours, at six p.m. Zak is the bureau's headache. I haven't got time for . . ."

"Shut up, Stone."

He said it quietly, so I did.

"What?"

"Couple of days ago, a neighbor reported to the Cumberland County sheriff that there seemed to be people at the Hellfire Club again. They sent over a deputy. Zak was there, and the deputy tried to arrest him. He shot the deputy and fled. The deputy managed to radio for help, but by the time they got there, Zak was long gone."

"Why are you telling me this, Captain?"

"Because you need to know. Now just shut up, John, and listen to me."

"Okay."

"The deputy said he was not driving a bike. He drove away in an old-model Cherokee. Looked like a '95 model. Green." He paused. My head was spinning. I had a flash in my mind of arriving at the club. Bikes. A Land Rover. A green Cherokee. The captain was saying, "Now, I am half-inclined to hand this over to somebody else, John . . ."

"Don't do that, Captain."

"Can you hold it together?"

"Yes."

"One of your neighbors called in earlier today. The message did not get to you because it was left on your desk, and you have barely been at the station house."

"What did the message say?"

"There had been a suspicious-looking man, looked like a Hells Angel, banging on your door. He left driving a green, early-model Cherokee."

"Son of a bitch."

"We put out an APB. The car has been spotted."

"He was parked behind the precinct. In the Rite Aid parking lot."

"Today?"

"When Dehan was abducted. Near the car where her phone was taped. Where is the Jeep now?"

He heaved a huge sigh. "At an old, abandoned church, at Jones Point, on the river. It's opposite Peekskill . . ."

"I know where it is. I'm on my way there."

"John, do not go. The bureau has this."

"Fuck the bureau!"

"*What?*"

"I said I trust the bureau. You're breaking up, Captain. Gotta go."

I hung up and switched off my phone.

TWENTY

I took East 222nd across to the River Bronx Expressway. Then I broke the speed limit all the way to Elmsford. There I took I-287 across the Tappan Zee Bridge and scorched through Nyack onto the Palisades Interstate Parkway. I came off at Stony Point. After that I had to slow down, because the road wound and twisted, meandering among secluded clapboard houses and woodlands.

The light was beginning to fade, and the roads were wet and shiny with drizzle, but I couldn't afford to drop below fifty. The Jag gripped the road like it was nailed to it, and I prayed to whatever gods look after reckless cops that I wouldn't encounter anyone on the road around the next bend. Because I would not be able to stop.

Then, at Tomkins Cove, I was suddenly out in open countryside. I floored the pedal and did a hundred and twenty along the riverbank. I came to a fork in the road and slammed on the brakes. I knew where I was. There was a parking lot on the left, and I pulled in and stopped. I climbed out of the car and cocked my automatic. The way I was feeling right then, Zak would be a very lucky man indeed if he went away for life.

He'd be a lucky man to make it to the trial.

I moved down the road at a steady run. There were dense areas of trees and bushes on either side, and though they were bare of leaves, they were thick enough to provide cover in the failing light. I came in sight of the church and hunkered down behind a tree. The road forked again just ahead, and the left branch curved in a crescent through an open esplanade of grass, where the old church stood with gabled roof and spire. Parked out front, on a patch of muddy lawn across the road, were a green Cherokee and a Ford pickup. That meant I was dealing with six of them, tops.

Even if the main entrance to the church was open, which I doubted, going in that way was not an option. I began to circle back, through the trees, to see if there was a rear entrance to the vestry. I covered about a hundred and twenty yards at a ducking run, to what looked like a toolshed set about thirty yards back from the front of the church. It was dusk turning to dark, but I could see a red door. There were no windows.

I paused to think. I needed some kind of plan. The Feds would arrive at some point, and when they did, I knew exactly what was going to happen. Storming a stone church with no windows and only two doors was not easy, and the whole damn situation would degenerate into some kind of Waco-style stand-off. I could not afford to do that.

I checked Dehan's phone. I had less than two and a half hours. That meant one thing: my plan was to go in and get her. There was no time for anything else.

I readied myself for the sprint to the door and heard a soft click in my ear.

"Freeze. Put down the gun and tell me who you are."

My mind flashed through the options. If he was one of Zak's Angels, he wouldn't be asking me who I was. He'd just blow me away. That meant this was a Fed. I said, "I'm Detective John Stone. I'm here to get my partner out of that church alive before you Feds set up a Waco circus here, and I am not going to put down my gun. Are we clear?"

The guy sighed. "At least show me your badge."

I showed him.

"I can't let you go in there, pal. They're on their way. Your captain is with them, and the instructions were very clear. 'When Stone arrives, clap him in irons if you need to, do not let him go in.'"

I turned and looked at him. If he was standing up, he would be six six at least. He'd probably been a quarterback at college, and he looked as tough as concrete. He smiled and held out his hand. "Agent King."

I gave him my best rueful smile and shifted my automatic to my left hand. He thought I did it so we could shake. He was wrong. I did it so I could land a right cross on his jaw that would have put an elephant to sleep. He fell back with a soft splat in the wet grass, and I sprinted to the door. I had about five minutes, if that, before the circus arrived. I tried the handle and was not surprised to find it was locked. I took off my jacket and wrapped it around the barrel of my gun. It muffled some of the sound when I blew out the lock. I waited. Nobody came storming out, so I inched open the door and edged in.

I was in a short corridor. There were a couple of doors that looked like storerooms. At the end, the passage opened out into the nave of the church, and I could see a few rows of pews. From the left, there was a soft glow of light. I moved forward a couple of feet and peered around. There was the altar, and beyond it, in the transept, somebody had some candles burning, and I could hear the murmur of voices. I waited, hoping to hear a female voice. I didn't.

What I did hear was the thud of a chopper and the wail of sirens. Then I heard cussing and swearing, and I saw six Angels, all armed, run toward the main door at the far end of the church. There was a gallery above the door that I figured had room for about eight pews. At the back there was a window. The access to the gallery was via a short wooden staircase. Four of them took positions covering the door, and Zak and another scrambled up the stairs to look out of the window.

Even these guys were not stupid enough to forget they had a back door. I had a matter of a few seconds in which to decide what I was going to do.

Zak made a noise like a wounded pterodactyl that turned out to be a laugh. "We got a whole fuckin' army out here, boys! We are gonna have a *bloodbath*!" He leaned over the gallery and said, "Hey! Gas, Lenny. Take the back door." He turned back to the window as Gas and Lenny started moving down the center aisle toward me.

It was now. It had to be now. And as I thought that, the bullhorn started bellowing outside and Zak started shouting abuse back at it. I didn't aim for the approaching Angels. I aimed for the two at the front door. I figured the shot at twenty yards and aimed for the middle of the body. They were big bodies; it was hard to miss. I squeezed off four rounds—two double taps. With all the noise of the chopper and the bullhorn, they went down in silence.

Gas and Lenny saw the flames spit from the muzzle of my gun in the shadows, and for a moment they stood staring. They were only about ten yards away. I'm a good shot and I was real mad, so they got it between the eyes.

Then I ran. I sprinted along the side aisle and took the stairs two at a time. Zak had smashed the window and was leaning out, screaming abuse at the Feds outside. His pal looked at me in astonishment as I came up the stairs. Instead of shooting me, he stared down into the nave, looking for his pals, trying to understand. Maybe Mephistopheles could explain it to him when he got to hell. I shot him through his right eye, and he sank to his knees. Zak turned. He brought his shotgun around, but it was too late. I drove my fist into his belly, and we both went crashing to the floor.

I don't know if he was tough, or if he just enjoyed the pain. A normal guy would have been curled up in the fetal position vomiting. He just grinned, grabbed me by the throat, and started strangling me. It's surprisingly difficult to punch somebody when you are lying down, especially if they have their hands around your throat. So I didn't even try. Instead I forced my elbow between his arms, placed it on his eye, and leaned on him, hard. He screamed and thrashed his legs like a speared fish, then let go of my throat and started tearing at my hair.

Somehow, he scrambled out from underneath me and connected two powerful blows that sent me reeling against the wall. Outside, the bullhorn was still going. Zak came at me. I drove my fist into his belly again, but he didn't seem to feel it. He grabbed me by the scruff of the neck and hurled me toward the edge of the gallery. I staggered and stumbled, and he rushed at me, screaming. We collided and fell against the rail. For a moment I was going over. I clawed at his beard with my left hand. He backed away and pulled me back with him. I came forward, and as I did so, I smashed my right fist into his head.

However high you are, there are laws of physics that still apply. I saw his eyes roll and his legs wobble, and I laid into him until he fell on the floor. Then I cuffed him and ran down to the south transept, reaching for my cell. I dialed the captain.

"Stone! Where the hell are you?"

"In the church. Dehan isn't here." I swore violently and kicked a few pews. "Check the pickup and the Cherokee."

"But . . . who's in there?"

"They're all dead, except Zak."

I hung up and ran up the stairs. I had a few seconds before the 7th Cavalry came pouring in. I grabbed Zak by the scruff of his neck and woke him up with two powerful slaps. His eyes stared at me like animated saucers. I leaned down real close to him and snarled, "You have fifteen seconds, Zak. Where is she, or I will gut you with a blunt screwdriver. *Where is she?*"

His head flopped back, and he closed his eyes. "I killed her, man. Out by the fucking lake at Camp Kaufmann."

I stared at him. The church was rocking. I said, "No, you haven't had time."

He narrowed his eyes at me. "What the fuck are you talking about?"

"*Detective Dehan!* Where have you put Detective Dehan?"

He laughed. "Oh dear, have we lost Detective Dehan?"

There were feet running, tramping up the stairs, and a voice saying, "Put the gun down, Detective. Put the gun *down!*"

I half turned. There was a special agent pointing a gun at me, and the captain was coming up the stairs behind him. I put my gun in my holster and stood.

"Go fuck yourself, Special Agent. I just did your goddamn job for you."

I pushed past the captain and went down the stairs to the nave. The place was crawling with Feds who kept giving me quizzical looks. They were crouching over the bodies and sealing off the area. The agent I had just told to fuck himself came down with the captain. He showed me his badge. "I am Special Agent Turner. Did you kill these men?"

"No, it was the tooth fairy. Of course I killed them."

"There will have to be an investigation, Detective Stone . . ."

I burst out laughing. "Into how I used excessive force against six heavily armed Hells Angels who were about to open fire on federal agents? Be my guest. You done?"

His face flushed. "There is also the matter of the agent you knocked out!"

"He was pointing a gun at me. *Now* are we done? Because right now there is the matter of my partner, who will be murdered in two hours!" I turned and pointed at Zak, who was being led down the stairs. "And *that* man knows where she is!"

He leered at me as he was led past.

Turner scowled at me. "Make yourself available, Detective."

"Screw you, Special Agent!"

He ignored me and walked out.

We were silent for a moment. Then the captain said, "Stone, professionally, I cannot condone what you have done. But I get it, and I will back you all the way."

I stared at him.

"Where is she, Captain?"

TWENTY-ONE

I SAT ON THE STEPS OF THE CHURCH. THE DRIZZLE HAD turned to freezing rain. The wet blacktop beyond the grass pulsed with red and blue over a silver sheen. The meat wagons had arrived, and the gurneys made a grim procession, driven by men and women in glistening masks, ferrying the dead out of the church, while the Feds set about the business of minutely analyzing the crime scene.

I was staring at Dehan's phone. I had one hour and fifty minutes. I hadn't a single lead. And with every passing minute, the chances of finding her alive diminished. I kept asking myself, where was she going? Why had she left the observation room?

I flipped to her call register. Five minutes before I'd finished the interrogation with David, she had received a call from a cell phone. If it had been Zak or Peter, she would have put her head in the door and told me. The fact that she hadn't meant it was either private or she didn't think it was important. Somebody she'd met recently? A guy she'd given her number to? But if she didn't think it was important, why did she leave the observation room? I tried to visualize Dehan walking out of an interrogation to talk to a guy. It didn't work. That wasn't the Dehan I knew . . .

And so I kept going, around and around in circles.

I looked over at Newman, talking to a Fed.

"Captain!" He approached me across the muddy grass. I showed him the phone. "This number called Dehan five minutes before she was taken. Two gets you twenty it's a prepaid, unregistered phone, but can you have it checked anyhow?"

He nodded and reached for his cell. "Sure."

I scrolled down through her calls as he walked away. I could hear him saying, "Yeah, trace a number for me, will you . . . ?"

There was no record of that number having called her before or of her calling that number. So the chances of the call being related to some private, personal matter were slim at best. Which meant it was a call related to work, to this case . . .

Slowly, as the rain fell on the gleaming cars and vans and the blacktop, and the icy air crept off the river and felt its way into my muscles and my blood, the clear, simple reality began to dawn on me. This son of a bitch was all about showing you things the wrong way around. His game was to take the obvious and show it to you so that it looked like the opposite of what it was. The photograph was classic. That photograph was like a picture of him. It represented everything that he was about. Everything was the wrong way around and focused on the wrong person. That was him. That was the essence of how he operated.

All along, the focus had been on David. All along, the picture had been framed around David, with him as the focal point. But who was the photographer? Who was holding the camera and focusing the lens? Who had created the picture in the first place? Somebody nearby. Somebody clever. Somebody disciplined and organized. Somebody who was almost a mirror image of David.

I stood and walked to Turner, who was standing by one of the bureau vans.

"You got a computer I can use?"

He looked at me like I was a piece of shit somebody had failed to clean up. I sighed.

"Detective Dehan will die in less than two hours if I don't

find out where she is. I may have an idea, but I need a computer. Will you let me use one or not?"

He made an ugly face that even his mother would have wanted to slap. "I'm busy."

I put my hand on his shoulder and leaned real close to his ear. "Turner, if you don't give me a computer, first I am going to blow your testicles off. Then I am going to sue you for Detective Dehan's wrongful death. I will take your job, your house, your car. I will break up your marriage, and I will make sure your kids hate your miserable guts for the rest of their lives. I will not stop, I will not desist, until I destroy you completely."

I pulled back a little so he could look into my eyes and know that I meant it. He stared at me. I wasn't shit anymore. Now I was a freak. I was moving up in the world. He leaned into the van and said, "Jerry, give me my laptop."

He typed in his password and handed it to me. "I'll check the history. Don't do anything you might regret."

I held his eye and tried to suppress the rage that was building inside me. "Right now, Special Agent Turner, you need to be worrying about whether I am going to do something *you* may regret. Stop waving your fucking dick around and get on the case."

I took the computer into the church and started searching the land registry. It didn't take long before I found what I was looking for. Peter Smith had a second house, on Jackson Avenue, in the Bronx. I knew the street. I knew the house. It was rough. Not what you would expect from Peter.

I went to call the captain, but he was coming for me. I said, "There is a chance she is at this address. We need to get there fast, and we need a warrant to search the property."

"What property?"

"It's a house on Jackson Avenue. It belongs to Peter Smith, the guy who owns the lockup. To be honest, I have never liked him as our guy, but . . ." I shook my head. "Unless I'm missing something really obvious, it's either David or Peter, and now we know it's not David. We are out of options."

He held up his cell. "That number you asked me to trace? It was Peter's cell."

"*What?*"

"Let's go. I'll call Judge Sanders for search warrants on that place and his house."

I drove fast. We were both silent. I was thinking hard as we roared down the darkened highway. In my mind, I could see almost the whole thing now. It all made perfect sense, and I was raging at myself for not having seen it before Dehan got taken. It had been obvious from the start. But that was how this guy operated. His genius, if that was what it was, was to invert things, turn them into negatives of themselves, show them back to front.

The only time the captain spoke was as we streaked between two sixteen-wheelers. "I do appreciate the urgency, John. But it would be useful to arrive there alive."

I glanced at him and nodded, but I didn't slow down. It was a journey that should have taken forty-five minutes. It took us barely half an hour.

There was a patrol car waiting at the house. Officer Sanchez and his partner climbed out as we pulled up. He handed the search warrants to the captain. I ran up the stairs, hammered on the door, and leaned on the bell. There was no reply. I took out my piece and shot out the lock.

I heard Sanchez say, "Woah!" I didn't give a damn. I ran in. Captain Newman, Sanchez, and his partner were right behind me. There was a short passage that led to a kitchen at the back. A door on the left opened into a living room, and on the right, stairs led to an upper floor.

I pushed into the living room while the captain went to the kitchen and the patrolmen went upstairs. The living room was shabby and seedy. There was a sofa, and two armchairs in brown vinyl. A TV was positioned opposite the sofa, and stacked next to it on the floor was a collection of pornographic DVDs. There was a cheap dining table and four chairs, and beyond them a set of French doors looked onto an overgrown back garden. Whoever used this place didn't use it for gardening.

The captain came in from the kitchen. "Nothing."

Sanchez called down from upstairs. "Clear, Detective!"

I went up and had a look around. There were two bedrooms and a bathroom. In the bathroom, there were patches of mold on the walls. The mirror was speckled, and the floorboards creaked underfoot.

In the master bedroom, there was a large king-size bed. It looked like IKEA, new. The sheets were fresh and clean. There was a cheap carpet on the floor, but that was also new, as were the drapes on the window. The walls seemed to be recently painted. I looked in the wardrobe. The only clothes were women's BDSM role-playing costumes.

In the second bedroom, the paper was peeling off the walls. There was a single aluminum-framed bed. The sheets were old, stained, and frayed. It was hard to imagine Peter in a place like this. And once again, I had the feeling that the picture was wrong. I had it all—almost. But something was missing.

I ran down the stairs and went out to the back garden. The captain followed. Sanchez flipped a switch in the kitchen and an outside light came on. Around the side of the house, I found a flight of stairs that led down to a door. I glanced at the captain. My heart was pounding.

"It's a cellar."

I pulled out my piece to shoot out the lock again, but Sanchez said, "Detective?"

I looked up. He was holding some keys. "They were by the light switch, in the kitchen."

I nodded. I unlocked the door and went in, shouting, "*Dehan! Dehan!*" There was only an empty echo.

I hit the switch by the door. There was a boiler against one wall, pipes running across the ceiling, boxes, a washing machine and dryer. I went to every wall and knocked on each one to see if they were hollow. They were all solid. I examined the pipes for scrape marks made by cuffs. There was nothing there. She was not here. She had never been here. I felt the cold, white fingers of despair clenching inside. The captain, Sanchez, and his partner were staring at me.

"She's not here, Stone."

I checked Dehan's phone. We had half an hour.

The captain spoke again. His voice sounded too loud in the empty cellar. "She's not here. So she's got to be at his house. And if she's not there, we'll make him tell us where she is."

I nodded, but I couldn't shake that feeling—the feeling that I was missing the main point, like when I kept looking at the photograph.

"We are missing something."

He wasn't listening. He made for the door. "Let's go and pull this son of a bitch in."

I followed him back up the stairs. We climbed into the Jag, and the patrol car led the way through the darkness and the rain, with its siren howling and its lights pulsing. We came fast down Bruckner Boulevard and turned in to Revere with the tires skidding and screeching on the wet road. We had ten minutes.

His vehicle was parked out front, and there was light in his windows. I jumped out of the car and ran. I hammered on the door and heard voices inside. Peter pulled the door open. He looked scandalized.

The captain was showing him the warrant as I pushed past him and ran up the stairs. I could hear Newman asking him, "Where were you this afternoon at three p.m.?"

I went into the master bedroom. I could hear Sanchez and his partner coming up behind me. I went onto the landing, pointing back into the bedroom. "Every drawer, under the bed, every inch for any trace of her."

I checked the other bedrooms and shouted, "When you're done in there, check the other rooms. Every damned inch!"

I ran down the stairs. The captain was still talking to Peter.

Peter was saying, "I have been here all afternoon. My wife will attest to that!"

I butted in. "Is there a cellar?"

He still looked scandalized. "What?"

"*Is there a cellar?*" My voice rang out loud and ugly. I grabbed him by the scruff of the neck. "*Is there a goddamn cellar?*"

He looked terrified. Jenny had her hands over her mouth. He said, "Yes," and led me to the kitchen. The cellar door was not locked. I switched on the light and ran down. Peter and the captain followed. As with the other house, it was one large room. There was a boiler against one wall. There was a washing machine and a dryer. There were boxes stacked here and there. I went to each wall, tapping, listening for a hollow echo. I felt sick. My heart was racing. I checked my phone. I had two minutes.

Suddenly, something snapped, and I lunged at him and grabbed him by the throat with my left hand. I had my automatic in my right, and I thrust it in his face and screamed at him, "*Where is she? Tell me where you have her or I swear I'll blow your fucking brains all over the walls!*"

The captain was shouting at me, "John! John! Get a grip!"

Peter had his eyes closed and was repeating, "*Oh God! Oh God! Oh God!*"

Then there was a noise. It was loud and jarring, and we all stopped and stared at each other. My skin went cold and pasty, and I felt my hair prickle. It was an electronic beeping, like an alarm clock on a cell phone.

I heard myself say, "No . . ."

I pulled Dehan's phone from my pocket. The time was up.

And in that instant it hit me.

I ran.

I ran scrambling up the stairs. I could hear the captain shouting after me. I ignored him and bolted through the house. Jenny was there, still with her hands over her mouth. I leapt down the steps and sprinted along the wet pavement toward Barkley Avenue, with the rain drenching my hair and my face. It must have taken me twenty seconds, no more, but each stride was an eternity. I skidded and fell on the corner. Scrambled to my feet and ran for the alley.

Another agonizing twenty seconds. My lungs were screaming. My heart was pounding so hard I felt my head was going to explode. I was screaming her name through the rain. I stared at the lockups. Which one?

"*Which one?*"

I blew the lock off Peter's and hauled up the roller blind. It was empty. I ran across to the GCS units. I blew off the lock on the first and dragged up the blind. There were only computers. I went to the next, took aim, and that was when I smelled it. I froze. Then I put on the safety and hammered the padlock with the butt of my gun. It sprang, and I dragged the door open.

There was a canister of butane gas. There was a valve with a timer attached. It was hissing loudly. Dehan was lying on the floor. Her wrists and ankles were tightly bound with duct tape. She had tape across her mouth. Her eyes were closed, and her skin was cold and pale like marble.

I bit back the tears and whispered, "*No . . . Oh no . . .*"

I turned off the gas and picked her up in my arms. I carried her out into the rain and laid her on the ground. I pulled the tape from her mouth and felt for a pulse in her neck. There was nothing. She was dead. I pumped her chest, pinched her nose, and blew hard into her mouth. Pumped again on her chest. Blew hard into her mouth. Pumped.

I pulled my penknife from my pocket and cut the tape from her wrists, spreading her arms out to open up her lungs. I shouted at her, "*Come on, goddamn it, Dehan! Don't do this to me!*"

I pounded hard on her chest again, pumped up and down, put my mouth over hers, and blew hard and steady.

She made a horrible noise, like a car that won't start. Her eyes snapped open, and she gasped in great gulps of air. Then she rolled on her side and vomited, copiously. I stood and looked away, clenching my teeth and blessing the rain for hiding my tears, mixed with laughter and sobs of relief.

A figure was moving up the alley at a run. It was the captain. I shouted to him in a strangled voice, "She's alive. But we need an ambulance!"

He stopped running and pulled his cell from his pocket, striding toward us as he dialed. I turned back to Dehan and knelt by her side. She looked yellow in the limpid light. She tried a smile but didn't quite make it.

"I knew you'd come."

I picked her up in my arms and carried her back toward Barkley Avenue. I said softly, "Who was it, Dehan? Who did this to you?"

She looked up into my face and touched my cheek with her fingers. "I don't remember anything, Stone. Except I knew you'd come."

TWENTY-TWO

I HAD MY ASS ON MY DESK, AND THE CAPTAIN WAS sitting in Dehan's chair. It was nine p.m., and I had just got back from the hospital.

"How is she?"

"She's very sick, but the doctor said she'll make a full recovery in a day or two. She hadn't inhaled enough gas to cause permanent damage. But if I had been a minute longer . . ." I shook my head. "Hell! If I had shot the lock, neither of us would be here right now."

He smiled. "How many locks did you blow away today, John?"

"I guess I lost it."

"You two are a good team. You care about each other."

I shrugged. "What about Sanchez and his partner? Did they find anything?"

"Davis. Yup. In their bedroom, Sanchez found an envelope containing a silver David's star on a chain. On the back, it was engraved 'To Carmen Dehan, from Mom and Daddy, on her first birthday, May 9, 1991.'"

He tossed it on the desk. It was in a plastic evidence bag. I picked it up and looked at it. It was the one I had helped her put on in Oacoma.

"Anything else?"

"The duct tape you sent in? The piece that had her phone stuck to the guy's van?" I nodded. "It's the same as the stuff that was used to bind her ankles and wrists, and it has a clear thumbprint on it. Peter's."

I stared at him for a bit. "Just one?"

"That's all they could get at the lab." He studied my face a moment and decided to ignore my expression. "I've arrested him. He's in the cell downstairs talking to his lawyer. Whenever you want to interrogate him . . ."

I gave a couple of slow nods. "Yeah, I'll talk to him now."

We walked together to the interrogation room. As I was going in, the captain put a hand on my arm.

"I'll be in the observation room, John. You got your shit together?"

"Yeah."

"No more threats of violence. No more violence, or we lose the case."

"I know. I'm okay."

A couple of uniforms brought Peter in about five minutes later. He was cuffed and he sat opposite me. He looked very pale and very scared. His lawyer came in after him. He didn't look happy either. He sat next to Peter and said, "My client is going to present a complaint against the city for police brutality. Are you Detective Stone?"

"Yeah."

"The complaint will cite you specifically, Detective Stone."

"Fine. We are not here to discuss your civil suits, Mr. Smith. We are here to discuss your attempted murder of Detective Dehan."

"That is a lie and an outrage! I have never laid a hand on Detective Dehan, or anybody else!"

I held up a hand. "Let's take it one step at a time, shall we, Mr.

Smith? I know you are a methodical man, and you like to do things methodically . . . isn't that right, Peter?"

His lawyer put his hand on Peter's arm. "You don't need to answer that, Peter. Can we stick to the point, please, Detective Stone? My client has not been arrested for being methodical."

Like most lawyers, this one was going to be a pain in the ass.

"Have you any reason for *not* wanting to acknowledge that you are methodical and systematic?"

Before his lawyer could intervene, his vanity got the better of him. "I am a methodical and systematic man. What of it?"

"So you'll have no trouble telling me where you were yesterday afternoon at a quarter to three."

"I already told your captain, I was at home, working."

"Have you got anybody who can verify that?"

"Of course. My wife was with me the whole time."

"Yeah, see, I was afraid you were going to say that. Because I, personally, wouldn't believe a word your wife says in your defense, and neither will the jury, because she is so obviously terrified of you."

"What? That's ridiculous . . ."

"Is it? Why do you say that?"

"Why would my wife be terrified of me . . . ?"

"I don't know, Peter. Why would she be terrified of you?"

His lawyer spoke up. "Detective Stone, you are deliberately confusing my client, presenting his own question to him as though it were an admission."

"Do you inflict physical violence on your wife, Peter? Or only psychological violence?"

"Don't answer that."

He swallowed.

I went on. "I am just trying to establish why she is so scared of you."

"She *isn't!*"

"Okay, so you claim that you were at home at two forty-five."

"I don't claim. I *was* at home."

"So when you telephoned Detective Dehan, you called her from home?"

"*What?*"

"Peter, the question is a very clear, simple one. Did you telephone Detective Dehan from home at two forty-five yesterday afternoon?"

He was shaking his head and looking at me as though I was crazy. "I didn't call her from anywhere. I haven't telephoned Detective Dehan in my life. I don't even know her number."

I frowned at the file I had open in front of me. "But this is your number, isn't it?"

I slid the printout across the table and pointed to where it showed the last call to Dehan's cell. He stared at it a moment and then stared at me.

"But that's my *cell* number."

"Yes, Peter, that is your cell number. So when you made that call, at two forty-five, where were you?"

"No."

"What do you mean, 'no'?"

"You don't get it. I did not make that call. I could not have made that call. I haven't got my cell phone."

"What do you mean?"

"I lost my phone."

I laughed. "When was that?"

"A couple of days ago."

"How convenient."

"I am *telling* you! I lost my phone!"

"Well, then, Peter, perhaps you can explain something else to me."

"Dear God!"

"Have you ever seen this phone before?" I showed him Dehan's phone in a plastic evidence bag.

"Not that I am aware of, no."

"How about this duct tape?"

He shrugged. "It's duct tape."

"Have you ever seen that piece of duct tape before?"

"How the hell should I know? No! I haven't!"

His lawyer said, "How is my client meant to tell that particular piece of tape from any other?"

"Well, you see, Peter, the thing is that you very carelessly left your thumbprint on that piece of tape."

He narrowed his eyes at me. His lips worked like he was trying to form a word, like he couldn't find words to describe just how stupid I must be.

"You're lying, and you *know* you are lying."

I turned the bag over to show him where the dusted thumbprint had shown up. "While you're at it, Peter, maybe you can also tell me about this. What is this?"

I put Dehan's pendant in front of him. He stared at it, shook his head, and shrugged.

"It's a Jewish star. St. David's. What do you want me to say?"

"I'd like you to tell me if you have seen it before."

"No, I haven't."

"Then perhaps you can explain how it came to be in your bedside table drawer, and why it has your thumbprint on it."

His jaw actually dropped, and his eyes bulged. "You are *fabricating* evidence!"

"It's not that easy, Peter. Your lawyer will explain that to you."

The lawyer was staring at the evidence bags on the table. He looked annoyed. "Don't say anything else, Peter." He looked at me. "I need some time to talk to my client."

I collected up the evidence and closed the folder. I spoke to the lawyer for the first time. "I want to know about the arms in the lockup twelve years ago. I want to know about the skull in Oacoma and the torso at Miramar. I want to know about the trips to San Diego and L.A. I want to know how many girls he has killed and where their bodies are. You better start getting him adjusted to the fact that the game is over." I looked at Peter. "Tick tock, Peter."

I went downstairs and stood in the doorway, looking at the

interminable silver needles of rain falling listlessly into the puddles on the road, making ripples that went nowhere. The cars in the lot shone wet, but their windshields looked black and blind.

What was I not seeing? What was I missing?

My cell rang. It was the lab.

"Stone? It's Penny from the lab."

"Hey, Penny. What have you got?"

"The skull you sent in?"

"Yeah."

"I thought you'd like to know. We managed to extract enough material for a DNA match with the arms."

"That's great. Is it the same girl?"

"Yes, it was the same girl."

"Thanks, Penny."

I hung up and stood staring at the burnished copper ripples on the road. Somewhere in San Diego, a mother and a father still didn't know that their daughter was dead. I climbed the stairs, dialing the San Diego PD. I spoke to a Lieutenant Scott. I told him about the arms and about the skull, and that we had reason to believe that the victim was originally from San Diego. I said if he wanted, I could email him the details of the skull in case they had dental records they could match it with.

He thanked me, but he didn't seem awfully interested.

TWENTY-THREE

I WENT BACK TO THE INTERROGATION ROOM. PETER looked even more drawn and pale. His lawyer looked even more unhappy than he had before. He drew breath to speak, but Peter said, "You are making a *mistake*!"

His lawyer looked irritated. "My client is adamant that this evidence is false."

"So somebody is framing you, Peter?"

He nodded vigorously. "Yeah. You! You've had this case hanging there, unsolved, for twelve years because you are too damned incompetent to crack it, and now you want to close it, so you think, oh, we'll pin it on the guy who found the arms in the first place!"

I looked at his lawyer. "You should explain to your client just how difficult that would be."

He ignored my suggestion and asked me, "Have you any more questions, Detective?"

"Yeah. Tell me about the house on Jackson Avenue."

Peter closed his eyes and sank back in his chair. His lawyer was looking at him like he wanted to shoot him. "What is this now, Peter?"

Peter covered his face with his hands. "God! You people!"

"You had better explain. Did you take Dehan there?"

"*No!* For God's sake, Detective!" He stuck his arm out, like he was pointing at the house on Jackson Avenue. "It's a . . . a place where I go to relax. You've seen my wife, Detective. She is a very good, dutiful wife, but she isn't exactly setting the world on fire, is she?"

"I wouldn't know."

"Well, I can tell you, she is not! A man needs . . ." He stared at me, furious that I was forcing him to lose his dignity. "A man has certain needs! I use that house to satisfy those needs."

"Needs like killing and dismembering young women?"

"For God's sake! *No!*" He ran his fingers through his hair. "This is madness!" He sat forward. "Even you must be aware that there are a lot of prostitutes in that part of the Bronx. They provide me with a level of sexual satisfaction that my wife cannot."

"Did you pick up prostitutes in San Diego and L.A.?"

"Once or twice."

"Did you kill them?"

"*No!*"

"Have you ever been to Oacoma?"

"I have passed through . . ."

"Twelve years ago?"

"Almost certainly, more than once—why?"

His lawyer had given up and was just staring at his hands. I drummed the table with my fingers.

"Say I wanted to go with a really hot whore, could you recommend one?"

The lawyer raised his face to stare at me. Peter looked astonished. He hesitated. His lawyer turned to look at him. "Well, yes, a couple. But they're not cheap."

"How much?"

"The really good ones, you're talking about two hundred or two hundred and fifty an hour."

I smiled. "And how long would *you* keep going, Peter?"

His face turned serious. "Well, we've had sessions of a couple of hours on occasion."

"Couple of hours, huh? Five hundred bucks. And what do you get for that? What will they do for you?"

"A bit of bondage, domination . . ."

"You or them?"

"Depends what mood I'm in. Both."

"I want their names."

He heaved another sigh and wrote down a couple of names with phone numbers. I folded the paper and put it in my wallet. Then I took out my cell and took a photograph of him.

I was quiet for a moment, thinking. Then I leaned forward across the table.

"Peter, I don't know if you fully appreciate how much trouble you are in. There is very compelling evidence tying you to Detective Dehan's abduction and attempted murder. And that, in turn, ties you to the murder of a young girl in San Diego who disappeared during one of your trips out there. Her head turns up in Oacoma, where you passed through, and her arms turn up in your lockup."

His lawyer butted in. "That is purely circumstantial."

I nodded. "Yeah, but it is tied so tight to the abduction and attempted murder that any jury is going to buy the whole lot as a package, and you know it." I turned back to Peter. "Now, so far your only defense is that the cops are trying to frame you so they can get shot at a cold case. And that is not going to wash. So you need to be doing some real, serious thinking, Peter, either about a credible defense, or about a full, frank confession." I stood. "We'll talk again tomorrow."

I DROVE TO THE HOSPITAL. My head was aching, and the squeak and thud of the windshield wipers was like a cruel and unusual torture involving a fork, a chalkboard, and a troll with a hammer. I left the car in the parking lot and ran through the rain to the shelter of the entrance. I rode the elevator, wiping rainwater from my hair with my hands.

There was a cop sitting outside her door. I asked him if anybody had been to see her. He shook his head. "Not a soul, Detective."

I wondered briefly about her parents, her family.

Dehan was awake when I went in. She still looked pale and pasty, but at least she didn't look dead anymore. She gave me a feeble smile, and I sat down.

"I still don't remember anything."

I shook my head. "That's not why I'm here."

"Why are you here?"

I shrugged. "I'm going to pick up a couple of hookers, and I thought I'd drop in and let you know."

She gave her head a small shake. "I don't want any. I'm trying to give them up."

"Anyone you want me to call? Anything you want me to bring over?"

She blinked a slow blink. "I'll be back at work tomorrow."

"Let's play that one by ear."

I stayed awhile till her eyes closed, and then I stepped out. I shut the door and stood thinking. The cop looked up at me. "Don't let anybody in to see her except her doctor and the nurses. And whoever goes in, go in with them. I don't want her left alone with anyone—I don't care if it's the second coming of Mother Teresa. Got it?"

"You got it, Detective."

Back in my car, I called Peter's hookers, Zeta and Cherry Tipple. I told them I was a friend of Pete's and I wanted to meet them at the usual place on Jackson Avenue.

"How much is this party going to cost me?" I asked Cherry.

"Seein' as you's a friend of Pete's, we can give you a special price, honey."

"How special is special?"

"Two hundred an hour, fo' each of us luscious ladies."

I laughed. "You better be worth it."

"You won't have no complaints 'bout us, mistah."

"You come prepared. I'm into the same shit as Pete."

"No problem, big boy. See you in an hour."

I arrived early. The captain had arranged for the lock to be fixed. I dumped my coat on the dining table and stood looking at the room. It was hard to imagine how anybody could get aroused in a soulless, desolate place like that. I sat down by his DVD collection and worked my way through them. They were mostly bondage and domination. Not so much sinister as sad.

Twenty minutes later, the doorbell rang, and I went to let them in. Zeta was a tall, peroxide blonde making a brave, if misguided, attempt to look ten years younger than she was. What she was was forty and extensively renovated, with some of her original features, but not many. Cherry Tipple was buxom and dark. Her features were all original and plentiful, and once upon a time she'd had a pretty face, but life and people had turned it sour.

They pretended to admire me. I winked at them and told them to go ahead into the living room. I locked the door and followed them.

"Sit down." I gestured to the chairs, and as they sat I placed four hundred bucks on the coffee table. "This will take less than an hour."

Cherry said, "Already I'm not liking this."

I dropped onto the sofa and showed her the key. "The door is locked, Cherry. I'm a cop. And I need to ask you a couple of questions about Pete."

They looked at each other. Zeta said, "Pete? Who's Pete?"

"Pete may be a man who abducts hookers, kills them, and dismembers them, and then distributes bits of them all over the country." I pointed at the black window, speckled with dreary, orange raindrops. "Right now, as far as the world out there is concerned, I am just a John and you girls are showing me a good time. I'm happy for it to stay that way. But I need you to do me this favor. Do it, and you walk out of here with four hundred bucks, and maybe you help put a son of a bitch away who preys on ladies like yourselves."

They looked like I might have got through to them. I showed them the picture of Pete. "This your man?" They nodded. "What's his taste? What does he like?"

They looked at each other and giggled. Zeta said, "I put a collar 'round his neck and lead him around the room on all fours, while Cherry smacks his ass with a ping-pong bat."

I frowned. "That's it?"

Cherry shrugged. "A few variations sometimes, but that's basically it. Sometimes I ride his ass!"

They screamed with laughter.

"And that takes two hours?"

They both sighed. "You'd be amazed."

"Does he ever try to hurt you?"

"You kidding?" It was Cherry again. "I'd taser the motherfocker and stamp on his balls! No, he likes to be dominated. That's it. It don't go beyond that. And when we's finished, every time we have to listen to the fockin' little lecture about how we could be doing something so much better with our lives. One of these days, I *swear*! I am going to say to him, 'Yo! Motherfocker! How much money you make in the last hour? Coz I made two hundred bucks leading a stupid asshole around the floor on his hands and knees while he got his sorry ass whipped!'"

I drummed my fingers on the arm of the chair for a while. Finally, I said, "The money is all yours, ladies. You have a profitable evening." Cherry smiled as she picked up the cash.

"You sure you don't want something, sugar? You're all paid up."

"I'm good, thanks."

"Suit yourself."

"Be safe."

I let them out and watched them scuttle away into the shiny, wet darkness. I stood staring at my car. The windows looked real black. I thought of the unknown girl, the skull and the arms. I thought of her parents again. For them, until they were tracked down and informed of her death, she would be both dead and alive. Why did that thought keep haunting me? The thought that somehow it wasn't real until you *knew*.

And suddenly I thought I knew.

TWENTY-FOUR

IT WAS STILL DARK. THE ONLY SOUND WAS THE WET, desultory tap of raindrops on the windowsill and on the leaves of the trees outside. I turned my head and looked at the clock. The luminous green numbers seemed to be carved out of the blackness.

5:45.

The doorbell made me jump physically. It jarred my senses, stopped, and then jangled them again. I slipped out of bed, grabbed my piece, and ran silently down the stairs. I could see a silhouette through the frosted glass panel, backlit by the amber streetlight.

I moved to the side of the door, reached over, turned the handle, and yanked it open. Then thrust my automatic through the gap.

Into Dehan's face.

She grinned.

"Morning, Stone."

"What the hell . . . Do you know what time it is? Why are you not . . . ?"

She stepped in, closed the door, kissed me on the cheek, and said, "Thank you." She moved toward the kitchen, talking over her shoulder. "I slept like a babe. I woke up at half four and started getting flashes. I remember bits and pieces. I thought you'd want to know."

"At five forty-five in the morning?"

She was opening the coffeepot and glanced at the clock on the fridge. "It's five to six. Man up, Detective. Have a shower, you'll feel better."

I showered and dressed and came down to the now familiar bacon, eggs, toast, and coffee. I sat.

"You know, normally, I have a piece of toast and a cup of coffee."

"My grandmother would not approve." She put the plate in front of me. "One of my uncles said to her one day, 'Mammy, I'm gonna die!' She said, 'You'll die, but foist you'll eat!'"

I laughed. "Your paternal grandmother, I assume."

"Uh-huh."

"So"—I stuffed bacon in my mouth and spoke around it— "tell me whachou wemembah."

She looked disapproving and raised an eyebrow at me. "I got a call while I was in the observation room."

"Can you remember who from?"

"It was a woman."

I froze. Then smiled.

She went on. "She said she had vital information regarding the case of the two arms. She said she was right outside. She didn't want to come in because her life would be in danger if anybody saw her. She wanted me to go down to the deli on the corner.

"I got about halfway there. You know there's an exit from the parking lot on the left. A van came out and pulled up. It was dark. The driver beckoned me. Next thing I felt a brick wall hit my head, and that's all I remember."

"Do you remember waking up at any point?"

She nodded. "Twice. The first time I was on a mattress in the back of a van. I was cuffed to a rail. There was a night-light burning, and there was a camera mounted on a bracket near the ceiling, watching me. About five minutes after that, the light went out. I heard the side door open, felt a sharp jab, and I went out.

"The second time I woke up and I was bound hand and foot. I couldn't see anything, and I was lying on a concrete floor. I knew that couldn't be good. Shortly after that, I heard the hiss of gas, started to feel ill, and passed out."

I had finished mopping up the egg with the toast and was sitting back, sipping coffee, watching her in the dim light of the dawn.

I told her about Zak and about David, and about finding her pendant at Peter's place, and his prints on the duct tape. She listened carefully and thought about it. "So the woman is his wife." I didn't say anything, and she shrugged. "Obedient to the last, huh?"

I nodded. "That she is."

"Did you get a confession?"

"He swears he is being framed by the cops just so we can clear up an old case. His lawyer knows he's going down, but he won't accept it."

She was pensive for a bit. "It would be good to get a confession." She shrugged. "We have no idea how many girls he killed. How many moms and dads are there out there, wondering . . . ? It would be good to give them closure."

Closure.

The word sat there staring at me. "Not closure."

"Not closure?"

"No. Aperture. I'll tell you what we need. We need to open the box."

"What are you talking about, Stone?"

I stood and started collecting up the plates and the cups.

"I keep getting this nagging feeling." I carried them to the sink, then turned and rested my ass against the side to look at her. "This guy, he may be an asshole and he may have a below-average IQ, but he has a genius for making everything seem like something it's not. His whole thing seems to be, so long as you don't know the answer—the *truth*—everything is possible. It is time to open the box."

"What box? And how are you going to open it?"

"I need a couple of hours' research on the computer, and then a little help from my friends."

WE GOT to the station house at eight and went straight down to the cells. Peter was awake. He had a breakfast tray in front of him, but he hadn't touched it. He looked drawn and pale. He watched us with sullen eyes as we stepped in.

"What do you want now? To gloat?"

"Detective Dehan has started to remember."

He laughed a sour, twisted laugh and said, "Oh, I get it, now the evidence against me will be incontrovertible. Not only have you got manufactured fingerprints, now you have the eyewitness account of the victim!"

"Come on, Peter. We're going to talk to your wife."

He stared at me, and there was real hatred in his face. "You plan to destroy me completely. Not only the rest of my life in prison, but you are going to tell her my little secret. Can you leave me nothing?"

"Come on."

He stood. I cuffed him and we led him up the stairs. He looked surprised as we stepped out into the early-morning drizzle.

"Where are you taking me?"

"I told you."

"You're not bringing her here?"

"Nope."

He and Dehan climbed in the back, and we drove through the damp hiss of the traffic, along the Bruckner Expressway to Revere Avenue. I kept my eye on him in the mirror. He looked anxious and fretful. I pulled up in front of his house, and he and Dehan got out. We stood a moment in the spitting rain. I could see Bob and his wife looking out the window at us. Then Pete's door opened, and his wife stood there, staring, waiting.

I walked over to her and climbed the stairs. "Mrs. Smith. May I have the keys to your garage?"

"To the garage?"

"Yes, Mrs. Smith, to your garage."

She walked away, into the kitchen, and came back a moment later with two keys on a ring. She handed them to me. "What are you going to do with Peter?"

I didn't answer. I took the keys, and Peter and Dehan followed me down the side of the house. I unlocked the garage and hauled up the door. I looked back at Dehan. Across the road I could see that Bob and his wife had come out onto the porch.

I walked inside and scoured every surface. Peter said, "What are you looking for?"

His wife joined us, her hands clenched in front of her. She didn't look at her husband. I studied her face for a couple of seconds. It struck me that she had the same look of sick anxiety that he had. "You know, I keep going over in my mind what happened that night, twelve years ago. If only there had been a witness, somebody like David. Because David has an eidetic memory. What is commonly known as a photographic memory. Then it struck me. When Detective Dehan and I first came here, we had a chat with your neighbor, Mr. Luff, and he told us his wife not only has what he described as an elephantine memory, but she *notices* things."

Peter swallowed. "And what do you think she noticed . . . ?"

I smiled. "Oh, I think she noticed who turned up with a couple of arms in a plastic garbage bag. I think she noticed all sorts of interesting things. In fact, as they're here, why don't we go over and have a chat with them?"

The wet crunch of our feet made a strange echo in the early-morning street as we crossed the road.

"Good morning, Mr. Luff. Mrs. Luff. I wonder if we could take just a few minutes of your time?"

Bob was staring at Peter with an odd frown on his face. Then he switched to me and said, "Of course! Come in. I'll get chairs . . ."

Mrs. Luff ushered us in. She looked satisfied that we had at last accepted her invitation to tea. "Now come in, come in!" She pinched her lips and shook her head. "Peter! Jenny! What a mess! What a situation! Sit, sit, I'll make tea. Bob, chairs. Come on!"

Dehan and Mrs. Smith sat on the sofa. I sat in an armchair, and Peter sat in the other. Bob came scuttling in with two more chairs while his wife bustled efficiently in the kitchen. Peter's eyes were shiny, and he kept swallowing. Jenny was fiddling with the hem of her blue cardigan and looked like she might be sick.

Bob helped his wife bring in the tray, and between them they poured and distributed tea. Peter was looking at us like we had all gone insane. Maybe he was right. The setup had something of the Mad Hatter's tea party about it.

Mrs. Luff said, "You took the children to your sister's, Jenny?" Jenny nodded.

Mrs. Luff nodded back. "It was the only thing to do. They'll be okay there. She'll look after them."

Bob cleared his throat. "So, how do you think we can help you, Detective Stone?"

I sipped my tea. It was perfect. I set the cup down on the table and sighed while I organized my thoughts.

"It has been a fascinating and challenging case. Definitely not run-of-the-mill. I will admit, and Detective Dehan will back me up on this, I think, that we made a fundamental mistake, right at the start, that set us on the wrong course. It was almost catastrophic, and almost cost Detective Dehan her life."

Mrs. Luff tutted. "You were very lucky to have Detective Stone."

I raised an eyebrow at her. "The mistake we made was to call in one of the bureau's profilers and set about seeking a serial killer who fit the classic profile." I glanced at Peter. His eyes were like two needles with which he was trying to pin me to the chair.

"Somebody who was methodical, meticulous, narcissistic, domineering . . ."

I glanced at Jenny. She was staring hard at the hem of her cardigan, and I could see her lower lip curling.

"But our killer was a very different kind of man. He had what I described to Detective Dehan as a special kind of genius."

Bob and Mrs. Luff were both staring, engrossed. This was not how they had expected to spend the morning. I could see Peter's chest rising and falling. His face was flushed. I went on.

"His special genius was—*is*—to make everything seem to be what it is not. I first realized this when he sent us a photograph showing his supposed next victim. But in fact, he had reversed the photograph and the victim was not the woman who was highlighted in the picture, but the one concealed in the foreground."

Bob and Mrs. Luff nodded in perfect unison. Peter had turned to stare at Dehan. I went on.

"And he kept drawing my attention to a clock, advising me that time was passing. So I rushed to Detective Dehan's side. But again, it was an illusion. The abduction was timed for later, when I had relaxed my guard. All along . . ." I stood and walked to the window, to look out at Peter's house. "All along, this killer's aim has been to cast suspicion on other people—other people, all connected by just one thing. The lockups."

I turned and set my ass on the windowsill. I shook my head, as though I still couldn't work it out.

"It was when I realized that his genius lay in inverting things to make them look like the opposite of what they were that things started to drop into place. He had never made a mistake. Zak, like most people, believed that paper does not hold a fingerprint. But this guy *knew* that it did, and every note I received from him was as pure as the driven snow. So I was surprised when he started making careless mistakes." I glanced at Peter. He and Jenny were staring hard at each other. "Of course, the bureau profiler had told us that sometimes careful, organized killers will grow overconfident with successive, successful kills and start to make mistakes."

Bob leaned forward, frowning. "But?"

Mrs. Luff looked at him and nodded, like that's what she was going to ask.

"But he had already told me that he had been twelve years without killing. It was as though he had defeated the cops back then and had nowhere left to go. But when I turned up, nosing around, it fired him up again.

"The thing was, he had *not killed* for twelve years. So how could he become overconfident? He started out meticulous, and then suddenly, for no apparent reason, he became careless. And every act of carelessness pointed—just as the photograph pointed clearly and obviously at the wrong victim—every act of carelessness pointed at the wrong suspect."

I paused. There was absolute silence in the room, and five pairs of eyes fixed on me.

"We were meant to get it wrong with David, and we were meant to *realize* we had got it wrong with David, so that we could then be sure we had got it right with Peter."

Peter screwed up his face like his brain hurt, and Jenny began to sob. Bob and Mrs. Luff were goggling, with eyes and mouths like six perfect zeroes. Peter exploded, "What the hell are you saying, Stone? It *was* David after all?"

I laughed. "Oh, we could have! We could have gone around the mulberry bush again! But the chances of David having a female accomplice were slim, to say the least. No, I realized I needed to back up and look at who was *creating* this picture. Who was the artist, the painter, or photographer who *did not appear* in the picture?"

"What does that mean?"

I shrugged. "Well, the first thing, and this actually saved Detective Dehan's life, was Schrödinger's cat."

Bob looked surprised. "Schrödinger's cat?"

"Yes, you actually drew my attention to it on the first day, when we were visiting you. Schrödinger's cat was a thought experiment, intended to illustrate that the Copenhagen interpretation of Heisenberg's uncertainty principle was wrong. In this thought experiment, a cat is locked in a box with a device that at some unknown point will release a poison. If we follow the Copenhagen interpretation, until the box is opened, the cat is both alive and dead. Once we open it and we *know*, then the cat is *either* alive *or* dead. And you said to me on that day, Bob, that the lockup with the arms in it reminded you of Schrödinger's cat." I paused, staring at him. "And it was when I remembered that, that I realized Dehan was in one of the lockups, with a timed device. And of course, I was right."

There was total silence in the dull gray of the morning light. Bob suddenly said, "I am so glad I was able to help."

"So am I. Because I have to confess, I have been behaving in a rather bizarre manner recently. Peter will attest to that, won't you, Peter? I have actually been going around *smelling* people's shoes. For example, Bob, I notice that you wear rather exquisite, hand-made Spanish shoes."

Bob and Mrs. Luff both stared down at his feet. He gave a small laugh. "Yes, it was actually Peter who introduced me to them. I have always admired Peter's unfailing good taste and his relentless determination always to have the best."

I smiled. "Even when he doesn't deserve or appreciate it. He acquires these things, doesn't he, Bob? And then he doesn't value them." Bob looked blank and I held out my hand. "Call me crazy, but I do love the smell of good Spanish leather. There is nothing like it. May I, Bob?"

"May you what?"

"Smell your shoes."

"You want to smell my shoes?"

"Please."

Everybody was staring like they were following a tennis match. After a moment, he took off his shoes and handed them to me. He looked really uncomfortable. "Really, Detective, I don't know what you hope to . . ."

"Humor me, Bob, it is just a small demonstration." I briefly sniffed the soles and carried on talking. "You see, when I stopped looking at the pictures that the killer was feeding me, I started looking further afield, and I began to discover interesting things like, for example, the fact that you do not work. You live on a pension paid to you by your ex-employer after an accident at work incapacitated you. You worked, back then, as a master butcher at the Manly's chain of superstores."

"That's true, but . . ."

"It is a comfortable income, but not a handsome one. I discovered that you had originally bid for a house with a lockup. But the bank would not extend you that much credit. You were the odd one out. You had no lockup.

"And the more I thought of my killer as the person making the picture, the more I kept remembering this window here, staring straight out at Peter's house. Peter with the attractive wife whom he always left alone, Peter with the well-paid job, Peter with the house which was just a little bit bigger and better than yours. Peter, with the very lockup that you wanted to buy. Peter, whom you have detested and resented since the very day he moved in here, and you fell in love with his wife."

"What absolute rubbish!"

"Really? I think when we start questioning Jenny, another picture may emerge, about how you have hounded her for the last fifteen years, how every time her husband was away you would be there . . ."

Jenny spoke suddenly, and her voice was twisted with grief, frustration, and relief.

"Both of them! Him and his damned wife!" She turned to her husband. "I tried to tell you! How many times did I try to warn you? And all you could say was, 'We must keep the peace with the damned neighbors.'" She pointed a trembling hand at Bob and his wife. "They are crazy! But you won't listen! *Because you always know best!*"

I nodded. "Make a note, Peter, listen to your wife. Because having terrorized her into compliance, they repeatedly went to your house when you were out, stole your cell phone, stole your prints—probably using liquid silicon—planted Dehan's pendant in your drawer, and planted your prints on the duct tape and the pendant." I paused. "A jury might have bought it. But it was just a little too obvious, having been so careful, to suddenly leave two, perfect thumbprints on such perfect exhibits."

I turned to Bob and held up the shoes. "You wanted his lockup, you wanted his house, you wanted his wife . . . Your obsession extended as far as buying the same shoes online."

Bob was laughing. "It is true that I am fond of Jenny, we both are!" He gestured at his wife, who was smiling comfortably. "And I will not deny that Mrs. L. and I have often sat here and discussed how—forgive me, Peter—how wasteful Peter has been. He has been granted all the opportunities I never had, and frankly, he has thrown them away. And as I said, I—we—have always admired Peter's good taste. But I am afraid it is a quantum leap from there to inferring that I am a *serial killer* who gets his amusement from framing my neighbor for murder! *Please!*" He laughed.

I nodded. "I agree. And that is why I bought liquid iron."

"You did what?"

"I was expecting another one of your notes. You'd already visited me once, and I thought it was at least even chances that you'd be back. So I spilled Floradix liquid iron all over my porch. It was cold and damp enough that it would not evaporate. I planned to keep doing it all week if I had to, but as it was, at five a.m. you showed up to leave me your note. Liquid iron not only stinks, it shows up with luminol. Detective Dehan, have you got . . . ?"

She reached in her pocket and tossed me a small plastic spray bottle. She then got up, closed the drapes, and went to stand by the door. I sprayed the luminol over a patch of the sole. The room was dark enough to see the bright blue glow as it mixed with the oxidizing agent in the liquid iron residue. I held it up to show her. Then showed it to Bob.

Mrs. Luff turned to him and took his arm in both of hers. "Oh, Bob!" She gave him a cuddle and a squeeze. "I told you not to take it up again." He smiled ruefully at her, and she grinned. "But it was fun, though, wasn't it?"

He gave her a kiss. "Yes it was, Mrs. L. Worth every minute." He wheezed a laugh, screwing up his eyes. "Especially when you thumped her with your fist! What a punch! You should be in the ring, Mrs. L!"

Dehan was calling for backup, and I went to unlock Peter's cuffs.

EPILOGUE

I PLACED THE SIZZLING LEG OF SPRING LAMB ON THE table, removed the lid from the roast potatoes, and poured Dehan a glass of rather fine Rioja. Then I began to carve.

"Okay, Stone, admit it, this one had you foxed."

I nodded. "It did. I knew who it *wasn't* right from the start. I knew in my bones it was none of our three suspects, but what threw me was that there didn't seem to be any other option.

"Of course, with David and Peter, the red herrings were deliberate. But with Zak, it was just bad synchronicity. He came looking for me, not you, at just the time when Bob snatched you."

"So when did you start to think it was Bob?"

I loaded up my own plate, poured my wine, and sat.

"It's hard to say, because while I was beginning to suspect Bob, I was also coming around more to the view that it could, after all, be Peter. I have to admit that Bob was clever. Very damn clever." I raised my glass. "Here's lookin' at you, kid."

"Amen to that."

We sipped. "I guess when I realized that the photograph was not of Nancy Pierce, but of you, all the pieces started to fall into place and I began to get the feeling that the killer was outside the picture, creating a picture for us to look at. And then I remembered that impression I'd had the first day when we stepped into Bob's place. And that made me remember Bob talking about Schrödinger's cat. That pretty much clinched it. But I needed to be sure."

"That was clever, the Floradix liquid iron thing. That was smart."

"Hey, I'm a smart guy."

"Whatever. He confessed to six murders."

"And one attempted." I ate in silence for a moment, then said, "That did surprise me, them working together, like the Wests, and Brady and Hindley. She was the one who gathered the information about Peter, and then about Hank and David. And he put it all together and made the plans. They traveled together to San Diego and L.A., at the same time as Peter and David. Who would suspect a married couple? But they were too good. The investigation died, and the sport lost its appeal." I shook my head and sipped. "She is pleading not guilty. She says she was just helping her husband, like any good wife should. And in the end, it was she who stopped him killing."

"Talk about the fucking cuckoo's nest."

We ate in silence for a bit. Then I said, "Did I tell you Peter telephoned?" She glanced at me. "He wanted to apologize for having been unsupportive. He wanted to tell me he and his wife are seeing a marriage counselor, after they come back from a six-month cruise. He said this case has taught him a valuable lesson, that he should appreciate the good things he has in life."

"Wow." She sighed and set down her knife and fork. She picked up her glass and said, "Maybe he's right about that. You don't know how valuable the good things in your life are until you are about to lose them."

We held each other's eye for just a second. We touched glasses, and I said, "I'll drink to that."

And we did.

Don't miss GARDEN OF THE DAMNED. The riveting sequel in the Dead Cold Mystery series.

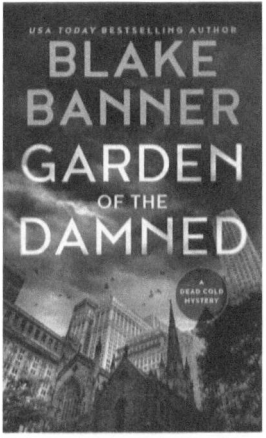

Scan the QR code below to purchase GARDEN OF THE DAMNED.

Or go to: righthouse.com/garden-of-the-damned

NOTE: flip to the very end to read an exclusive sneak peak...

DON'T MISS ANYTHING!

If you want to stay up to date on all new releases in this series, with this author, or with any of our new deals, you can do so by joining our newsletters below.

In addition, you will immediately gain access to our entire *Right House VIP Library,* which includes many riveting Mystery and Thriller novels for your enjoyment!

righthouse.com/email

(Easy to unsubscribe. No spam. Ever.)

ALSO BY BLAKE BANNER

Up to date books can be found at:
www.righthouse.com/blake-banner

ROGUE THRILLERS
Gates of Hell (Book 1)
Hell's Fury (Book 2)

ALEX MASON THRILLERS
Odin (Book 1)
Ice Cold Spy (Book 2)
Mason's Law (Book 3)
Assets and Liabilities (Book 4)
Russian Roulette (Book 5)
Executive Order (Book 6)
Dead Man Talking (Book 7)
All The King's Men (Book 8)
Flashpoint (Book 9)
Brotherhood of the Goat (Book 10)
Dead Hot (Book 11)
Blood on Megiddo (Book 12)
Son of Hell (Book 13)

HARRY BAUER THRILLER SERIES
Dead of Night (Book 1)
Dying Breath (Book 2)
The Einstaat Brief (Book 3)
Quantum Kill (Book 4)
Immortal Hate (Book 5)
The Silent Blade (Book 6)
LA: Wild Justice (Book 7)

Breath of Hell (Book 8)
Invisible Evil (Book 9)
The Shadow of Ukupacha (Book 10)
Sweet Razor Cut (Book 11)
Blood of the Innocent (Book 12)
Blood on Balthazar (Book 13)
Simple Kill (Book 14)
Riding The Devil (Book 15)
The Unavenged (Book 16)
The Devil's Vengeance (Book 17)
Bloody Retribution (Book 18)
Rogue Kill (Book 19)
Blood for Blood (Book 20)

DEAD COLD MYSTERY SERIES
An Ace and a Pair (Book 1)
Two Bare Arms (Book 2)
Garden of the Damned (Book 3)
Let Us Prey (Book 4)
The Sins of the Father (Book 5)
Strange and Sinister Path (Book 6)
The Heart to Kill (Book 7)
Unnatural Murder (Book 8)
Fire from Heaven (Book 9)
To Kill Upon A Kiss (Book 10)
Murder Most Scottish (Book 11)
The Butcher of Whitechapel (Book 12)
Little Dead Riding Hood (Book 13)
Trick or Treat (Book 14)
Blood Into Wine (Book 15)
Jack In The Box (Book 16)
The Fall Moon (Book 17)
Blood In Babylon (Book 18)
Death In Dexter (Book 19)
Mustang Sally (Book 20)

A Christmas Killing (Book 21)
Mommy's Little Killer (Book 22)
Bleed Out (Book 23)
Dead and Buried (Book 24)
In Hot Blood (Book 25)
Fallen Angels (Book 26)
Knife Edge (Book 27)
Along Came A Spider (Book 28)
Cold Blood (Book 29)
Curtain Call (Book 30)

THE OMEGA SERIES
Dawn of the Hunter (Book 1)
Double Edged Blade (Book 2)
The Storm (Book 3)
The Hand of War (Book 4)
A Harvest of Blood (Book 5)
To Rule in Hell (Book 6)
Kill: One (Book 7)
Powder Burn (Book 8)
Kill: Two (Book 9)
Unleashed (Book 10)
The Omicron Kill (Book 11)
9mm Justice (Book 12)
Kill: Four (Book 13)
Death In Freedom (Book 14)
Endgame (Book 15)

ABOUT US

Right House is an independent publisher created by authors for readers. We specialize in Action, Thriller, Mystery, and Crime novels.

If you enjoyed this novel, then there is a good chance you will like what else we have to offer! Please stay up to date by using any of the links below.

Join our mailing lists to stay up to date -->
righthouse.com/email
Visit our website --> righthouse.com
Contact us --> contact@righthouse.com

facebook.com/righthousebooks
x.com/righthousebooks
instagram.com/righthousebooks

EXCLUSIVE SNEAK PEAK OF...

GARDEN OF THE DAMNED

CHAPTER 1

FOR REASONS I COULDN'T REALLY PUT MY FINGER ON, IT was somehow appropriate. Out the window, April was coaxing the first tender green leaves from bare branches and withered twigs after a dark, cold winter. This seemed like a suitable counterpoint. I tossed the file onto the desk, narrowly missing my feet, and said, "This one looks interesting."

Dehan picked it up, leafed through it, and read the abstract on page one.

"John Doe." She smiled at me in a way that said she wasn't really smiling at me. "Good start." She carried on, "Aged about thirty, found in a dumpster at the corner of Lafayette and Bryant, in the Bronx. No papers, no ID. Clothes suggest a vagrant. Cause of death, a single gunshot wound to the back of the head, possibly a .38. No slug recovered and no blood found in the vicinity." She looked at me. "What makes this interesting?"

I frowned at her and spoke with some severity. "The fact that a young man got murdered."

She raised an eyebrow at me. "No. That is why we should investigate it. That doesn't make it interesting. So far it looks like a guy nobody cares about got whacked by another guy nobody cares about. You said it was interesting, why?"

"Look at the photographs."

She leafed through till she came to the photographs, three six-by-eights. She spread them on the desk and spent a couple of minutes staring at them. They showed a man of about thirty, in old, filthy clothes, lying facedown in a dumpster full of rubble and builder's trash. She shook her head. "Help me out. I'm not seeing it."

I gave a small smirk as I handed her my magnifying glass. "Have a look at his hands."

She stared at the glass a moment and then at me before taking it, then she looked at John Doe's hands. She sat back. "Okay, they appear to be manicured. You are observant, Sensei."

"And the hair. That is definitely a hundred-dollar haircut."

She leaned forward again and studied the photographs. She nodded. "So," she said and handed back the glass. "How do we figure this? He's in the neighborhood of Lafayette, maybe looking for a whore, he gets mugged . . ."

Even as she was saying it, she was seeing the flaws. I said, "Let's suppose he had a thousand-dollar suit that, by some fluke, happened to be the right size for our killer. So he kills him, takes his suit, his shoes, and his watch, plus his wallet. Why then go to the trouble of dressing him as a homeless person and dumping him in a dumpster?"

She looked back at the file.

"Single gunshot wound to the back of the head. Execution style." She shrugged. "These days any kid who wants to be in a gang is likely to shoot you in the back of the head just so he can boast he killed you 'execution style.'"

"True enough." I stood. "But if you look at the ME's report . . ." She leafed through to the report and read while I spoke. "You'll see that entry was at the base of the skull, and the exit wound was where the two clavicles meet above the sternum. Which means the shot was at about a ten- to twenty-degree angle. Like so." I demonstrated. "John Doe was kneeling, the killer was standing behind him."

"Execution style."

I nodded. "You haven't got a lot of dark back alleys around there. It's all mainly big, broad streets and open spaces. Plus we know they searched the area and found no blood, no slug. There was no bleeding inside the dumpster."

Dehan was watching me and nodding. "So it's clear he was killed somewhere else and then thrown in the dumpster."

"Right, so the killer gets him on his knees. Shoots him in the back of the head. He has either already made him strip, or he now strips off his clothes, and he dresses him as a vagrant. Then, presumably in the small hours of the morning, he takes him and dumps him. What benefit does the killer get from doing that?"

Dehan arched her eyebrows and spread her hands. "The benefit he actually got was that the case went cold almost immediately, and if you hadn't pissed off Captain Jennifer Cuevas it would probably have stayed cold."

"Hidden in plain sight." I nodded. "A guy nobody cares about murdered by another guy nobody cares about. So there is probably a missing persons report that relates to this guy, but nobody ever made the connection with our victim, because they assumed he was a vagrant. Let's find out who he is."

"Something else." She tapped the photographs. "Why that particular dumpster? Is it because it was close? Did they own it and they were planning a more thorough disposal, but it went wrong? Maybe it was just random, but I think it's worth looking into."

"Good, I agree."

The next couple of hours were drudgery fuelled by coffee. The dumpster belonged to a company called Hagan's Dumpsters, which was a spawn from a parent company called Hagan Construction, which in turn belonged to Conor Hagan, a guy known to be the head of a clan in the Irish Mob. Hagan's head office was on East 116th Street, one block from the Supreme Criminal Court. You've got to love the Irish and their sense of humor.

I was about to tell Dehan when she stretched out in her chair and sighed. "A lot of people went missing in New York in 2005. But when you filter out the women, guys over thirty-five and under twenty-seven, and people with a criminal record, you wind up with two, and one of them was a car mechanic."

I could hear the printer churning out a photograph. She stood and walked away, coming back a few seconds later with a photograph and a sheet of printed paper. She dropped the photograph in front of me and sat. This was our guy. She read from the printed sheet.

"Sean O'Conor, thirty years old at the time of his disappearance, an attorney specializing in human rights, junior partner at Stanley and Cohen, in Brooklyn. Also worked on a pro bono basis at the Drop-In Center, on Sheridan Avenue, a free representation unit funded by charities, which he helped to set up. There was him, David Foster, and Arnav Singh. The office closed down shortly after Sean disappeared.

"Parents, James and Kathleen O'Conor, apparently still living."

I sat back and scratched my chin.

"So, we have a case of an Irish human rights attorney from Brooklyn found, dressed as a vagrant, murdered execution style, in the Bronx, in a dumpster owned by the Irish Mob."

"Really?"

"Hagan Construction." I told her what I'd found.

"Where do you want to start?"

I stared at Dehan's face. It was a nice thing to stare at, and she stared back at me. It was a thing we did. Other people found it unsettling but it helped us to think.

"My gut," I said, "tells me whatever Sean O'Conor was doing in Brooklyn did not get him killed in the Bronx. I want to talk to his partners at the Drop-In Center, then maybe we have a chat with his mom and dad."

"My thoughts exactly, Sensei. You want to forage some food while I find out where Foster and Singh are?"

I left her to it and made for the deli on the corner.

CHAPTER 2

I GOT TWO BEEF ON RYE AND DEHAN MET ME OUTSIDE the station, sitting on the hood of my Jaguar. Not many women can sit on the hood of a 1964 Mark II and look good. Mostly you want to move them off so you can get a good look at the car, but Dehan looked like she belonged there. I handed her her sandwich and she began to unwrap it.

"David's office is in Manhattan, but he's at home today. Harbor Road, Oyster Bay, Long Island. I called and they are expecting us."

I opened the car. "I guess we can assume he isn't doing pro bono work anymore."

"Seems a safe bet."

We took the Bronx–Whitestone Bridge and then, at Cunningham Park, we turned east onto the Long Island Expressway and followed that as far as Jericho. The Jericho Oyster Bay Road was long and straight and leafy in the dappled sunshine, and there were cute houses hiding among the trees, with chimney pots poking out and leaded bow windows. It was like driving into a chocolate box.

We arrived at Oyster Bay and crawled through a sleepy town where it seemed almost everybody lived in a mansion, and the small houses were the ones with only five bedrooms and no tennis court. It was a tasteful place, but none had the gaudy ostentatiousness of Manhattan. You had the impression that poverty was not allowed here, not because it was immoral, but because it was in bad taste, like stretched limos and tiepins.

As we turned into Harbor Road, Dehan was looking around her with a kind of rueful air. "Jeez, I bet even the muggers here wear Ralph Lauren and say please and thank you."

"We have become cynics, Dehan. We devote our lives to fighting crime, but have you ever thought what it would be like if we won?"

She didn't answer for a moment, staring out at the rows of sweeping lawns, white picket fences, and rambling houses. "It never crossed my mind," she said at last, "that we might win."

He had an ample driveway, so I pulled in and parked beside his Porsche. As I climbed out and Dehan walked toward the front door, I glanced at the two cars. I thought mine fit better than his. It was less gaudy. Maybe I needed a house to go with my car.

David Foster had a polite Latin-American housemaid who opened the door to us. We told her who we were, and she led us out to the pool. It was not warm enough to swim yet, but it was pleasant enough for tasteful pre-prandial drinks on the patio. David was sitting at a white wrought iron table reading some documents, with what looked like a bone-dry martini by his elbow.

He looked up as we approached, smiled agreeably, and stood to greet us. We showed him our badges.

"I am Detective John Stone; this is my partner, Detective Carmen Dehan."

We shook and he gestured toward the table. "Please, take a seat. Can I offer you a drink? You are on duty, so perhaps some homemade lemonade?" He didn't wait for an answer, but turned and said, "Rosalía, *dos vasos de limonada, por favor.*"

She gave a cute little bow and walked back toward the house. We all sat. He was handsome in an Anglo-Saxon sort of way, with sandy hair and blue eyes. He smiled at Dehan and said, "When you called, you mentioned that you wanted to discuss Sean O'Conor with me. I haven't seen Sean for about twelve years. I am not sure what I can tell you about him, but may I ask what your interest is?"

Dehan glanced at me.

I said, "You worked together at the Drop-In Center, on Sheridan Avenue in the Bronx, is that right?"

He smiled. "Yes, there were three of us. They were good times. There was me, Sean, and Arnav . . . Arnav Singh!" He said it as though remembering their names was an achievement of some sort.

Dehan gestured around her. "It seems a long way from this."

"Oh, it is! But my uncle insisted on it. If I was going into his firm, he wanted me to experience life, and the law, at the sharp end. I'm glad I did it, and I'm glad it's over. But your interest is in Sean, not me, I gather. And I am still not sure why."

I asked him, "Do you recall what cases Sean was involved in back then?"

He frowned. "Only vaguely, and I am not sure I would be allowed to discuss them with you. If he discussed them with me in a legal capacity . . ."

"Privilege would extend to you, I understand that. The thing is, Mr. Foster, Sean was murdered, and we believe it may have had something to do with a case he was working on at that time."

His frown had become incredulous. "Murdered? Sean? But that's . . . grotesque! Poor Sean. What on Earth happened?"

Dehan said, "That is what we are trying to find out. I'm not a lawyer, Mr. Foster, but if he was murdered, surely you could be a little flexible."

He nodded. "Of course." He stared hard at the tabletop for a while. "Sean was a bit stereotypic, you know, very much the Irish firebrand. Always ready—a bit too ready if you ask me—to take on the big boys and strike a blow for the underdog." He looked at me and frowned. "That was what always surprised me. One day he just didn't turn up at the Center. Arnav and I stuck it out to the end of the month, but the driving force behind that place had always been Sean. So we just closed up shop and went our separate ways."

"Can you remember any particular cases he was working on just before he disappeared?"

He stared at me. "Is that why he disappeared? Because he was murdered? Twelve years ago?"

I nodded.

"Jesus . . . !" He sighed. "Yeah, his big thing at the time was a squatters' rights case. You should talk to Singh. He and Sean were thick as thieves. He was going up against a big construction company that wanted to evict, or was in the process of evicting, a bunch of people who were squatting in a building. The company wanted to knock down the site and develop it. Of course there were millions—tens of millions—of dollars at stake, but Sean's point was, quite correctly, that the rights of the people who were living there were being trampled on."

Dehan asked, "Can you remember the name of the construction company?"

He shook his head. "I can't, but I do remember him making a big thing at the time of the fact that they were Irish, like him. The whole Irish, Catholic thing was a big deal for him."

Rosalía came out with two glasses and a pitcher of iced lemonade. She poured us a glass each, left the pitcher, and went back inside.

I sipped and Dehan said, "You mentioned he was close to Arnav. You guys stay in touch?"

"No, he moved down to Washington. His thing was playing politics, not my scene. I get more than enough of that at work. But he was smart and ambitious, so he shouldn't prove hard to find. Then there was his church. Not Arnav, Sean."

I frowned at him. "His church?"

"Oh, yes! When I say to you that everything, and I mean everything, revolved around God, Jesus, and the Roman Catholic

Church, I am not exaggerating even a little. I don't know when he found time for his actual, real job, but he used to spend every spare moment he had at the church, doing everything from distributing clothes to running a soup kitchen, reading to little old ladies . . . you name it."

"Some guy." It was Dehan; she was looking skeptical.

"No, don't smirk, Detective. He was the real deal, an honest-to-goodness good guy. I try, let's face it, most of us try and do the best we can. We all care a bit, right? Not him. He was the genuine article. He really cared, completely. If you talk to the priest there, I am sure he will remember him."

I asked him, "What church?"

"St. Mary's, it was . . . let me see if I can remember . . . Lafayette. It was a big church. Old. You know, the ones that actually look like churches. You won't have any trouble finding it. The padre was Irish too. One of those 'O' names."

Dehan said, "O'Neil?"

He snapped his fingers and smiled. "That's the fellow. Father O'Neil, Padraig O'Neil!"

She nodded. "I know it."

Foster had got into his stride. "It's coming back to me now. He had a girl too. You should talk to her, although oddly enough she wasn't Irish. I think she was Venezuelan or Mexican maybe. Anyway, for sure she was Latin American. He was pretty sweet on her. I definitely remember that."

I asked, "Can you remember her name?"

He shook his head. "As I say, he and I weren't real good pals. I think I was too much of a WASP for his taste, Boston Brahmins, English ancestors . . . not his cup of tea. He was a nice guy, though."

We chatted a bit longer, finished our lemonade, and left.

Dehan closed her door and I sat drumming my fingers on the steering wheel. Dehan glanced at me. "Don't tell me, it's too easy."

I grimaced, turned the key in the ignition, and took off.

CHAPTER 3

JAMES AND KATHLEEN O'CONOR HAD A HOUSE IN Corona, just by the Flushing Meadows Park. It was a nice, detached place on 46th Avenue, which would probably have fit comfortably into David Foster's kitchen. As I pulled up in front of their gate, I paused a moment to think about relative values. I get deep like that sometimes. Dehan said, "You think the pool and the tennis courts are in back?"

I climbed out and looked at her across the roof of the car. The first green leaves of spring were coming out on the plane tree behind her. "Is that the whiff of sour grapes I detect in your voice, Dehan?"

She shook her head. "No, I'm just wondering, what didn't these guys do, that David Foster did do . . . ?"

"If your point is that life isn't fair, you're a little late. We already knew that."

She sighed. "I know."

I pushed through the gate and rang on the bell.

The door opened, and I looked down at a small woman of maybe five feet. She had a squint and short hair, jeans, a pink cardigan, and a mischievous smile.

"Can I help you?"

I showed her my badge. "Detectives Stone and Dehan, NYPD. Are you Kathleen O'Conor?"

"I am, what have I done now?" she said, and grinned.

I smiled back. "Nothing we know of, Mrs. O'Conor. We would just like a quick word with you and your husband, Jim. Is he in?"

"He's watching the TV, for a change. Come in." She walked ahead of us into the front room, speaking as she went. "Jim! Would you turn the feckin' TV off for five minutes? We have visitors."

We followed her in. There was an immensely tall man, with a shock of snow-white hair swept back from his face, folded into an armchair opposite the TV. He fumbled with the remote control, switched off the television, and levered himself to his feet. Once he had managed all that, he smiled. He must have been six foot six if he was an inch.

I told him who we were and they both told us to sit down. I watched Jim lever himself back into his chair, and Kathleen sat on the sofa, next to Dehan, with her feet barely touching the floor.

I sighed. "We need to talk to you about your son, Sean." I pulled the photograph Dehan had printed from my pocket and showed it to them. "Is this Sean O'Conor, your son?"

All the humor drained from their faces. Kathleen put her hand to her mouth and tears glistened in her eyes. Jim seemed to turn gray.

"Yeah. That's our son. Did you find him?"

"I'm afraid I have very bad news. Sean was found murdered."

Kathleen gave a scream. Her eyes went wide and she stared at me. Jim seemed to crumble. He sank back in his chair and put one massive hand over his eyes. Kathleen kept saying, "No! Oh, no! God no, please."

Jim spoke without opening his eyes. "When did this happen? Where has he been all this time? What has he got himself mixed up in . . . ?"

I took a deep breath, but it was Dehan who answered. "It

happened twelve years ago, Mr. O'Conor, but we were only able to identify the body this morning."

Kathleen's hands dropped into her lap. "What?"

Jim opened his eyes. "Twelve feckin' years?"

"Why were we not notified? Why was he not . . ."

"Twelve feckin' years!" Jim said it again, looking around the room as though he might find an explanation on the walls somewhere.

"I know it is hard to understand." Even as I said it, it sounded lame. "We were pretty surprised ourselves. But all his papers had been removed, and he had been dressed in the clothes of a vagrant. There was no possible clue to his identity."

Kathleen's face twisted and she started to sob. "Oh, God bless him, poor Sean!" Dehan put her arm around her.

Jim shook his head. His voice was a rasp. "Who would do a thing like that to my son?"

"That's what we mean to find out."

Dehan said, "We know this is really hard, but if you can help us, if you can answer a few questions for us . . ."

"We can come back later if . . ."

But they were both shaking their heads. Kathleen spoke into her handkerchief, twisting her nose. "I knew it. I knew he was dead. I said so, didn't I, Jim?"

"Ah, sure, we both knew, Kath. It's just, when you come face-to-face with it like that . . ."

"When you have it confirmed. And murdered . . . sweet mother of God, murdered . . ." She started sobbing again.

"Shall I make a cup of tea?" It was Dehan, stroking her back.

Kathleen gripped her hand and looked up into her face. "Would you, love?"

Dehan went out to the kitchen. I heard the cupboard doors bang and the tap hiss.

I said, "Did he ever talk much about his work with you?"

"All the feckin' time!" It was Kathleen, talking into her handkerchief again. She blew her nose. "It's all he ever feckin' talked about. His work, and the f . . . and the church."

Jim said, "He was very devoted to his work, and to the church, Detective."

"Do you recall what he was working on just before he disappeared?"

Jim nodded. "Oh, yes. How could I not? We both do, don't we, Kath?"

"Some feckin' squatters. Lazy feckin' no-good layabouts, want every feckin' thing handed them on a feckin' plate . . ."

She dissolved into tears. Jim watched her a moment, then turned to me. "They had taken over a building on Tiffany Street, in the Bronx. Big, five-story apartment block, so it was. Semi-derelict, no water, no electric, but there must have been some handy lads there 'cause didn't they get it all working? Illegal, like, but still . . ."

"And charge it to the feckin' honest taxpayer!"

"Not at all, Kath! Taxpayers had nothing to do with it."

"So you say!"

I coughed. "So, what did your son have to do with these squatters?"

"Didn't the landlord want to sell the site, so they could tear it down and make offices there? See, it was worth a hell of a lot more as offices than as apartments. So, one of the parishioners at St. Mary's, some down-and-out, one of them squatters, tells Sean they're being evicted, and doesn't he only go and start a case against the company that's selling the site. He claims agents for the company had taken rent from the residents, and therefore owed them compensation for evicting them."

"Can you remember the name of the company?"

He gave a dry laugh. "Well, that was another thing. It turns out, according to Sean, the company selling the property and the company buying the property are both owned by the same parent company, and they both have city officials sitting on the board of directors. It stank to high hell. And he was goin' after them, goin' for the jugular, so he was."

"Can you remember the name?"

"Remember it? I'll never feckin' forget it. Hagan Construction. That was the parent company, belonged to Conor Hagan, and you being a policeman, you'll be familiar with the name. Any Irishman who has lived in the Bronx is familiar with that name. Head of the Hagan clan, a big shot in the Irish Mob, a very dangerous man to cross." His bottom lip curled and he began to sob. "I never wished so bad that I'd had a coward for a son. May God forgive me, wasn't it his courage and his faith that cost him his life?"

Dehan came in with a tray, four cups, and a pot of tea. She set it down on the coffee table and started to pour. While she did, I sat back and stared out their bow window at the tree across the road.

Dehan handed me a cup and sat down next to Kathleen. I said, "So Sean was taking a case on behalf of the residents of this building on Tiffany Street, against Conor Hagan."

"Residents?" It was Kathleen. "Squatters and parasites, more like!"

A flash of irritation crossed Jim's face. "He was a good Christian, Kath. He lived by his faith . . ."

"And feckin' died for it!"

Dehan cut in before it escalated. "I believe he was active at a church in the Bronx."

Jim sipped. "St. Mary's. He was born in the Bronx, and we moved out here when he was a young lad, to get away from the crime. But we stayed in contact with the priest, a good man so he was, always ready to help, if he could."

"Father O'Neil. So Sean must have had friends at the church."

"Oh, he did that."

Kathleen smiled briefly. "And a lovely girl. God alone knows what she thought when he just vanished. Mexican, but a lovely, sweet child, as devout as he was. Isn't that how they met? In the soup kitchen, and delivering clothes during the bitter winter. They were both besotted, bless them."

Dehan asked, "What was her name, Kathleen?"

"God forgive me, I can't remember. Isn't it a shame? I only met her the one time when he brought her over for dinner. But it's that long ago, I cannot remember her name. Can you remember, Jim?"

He shook his head. "No. It was one of them Mexican, Spanish names. Maria, was it? Or Carmen . . . ? I don't recall."

I asked, "Any idea how we could find her or contact her?"

Kathleen looked at me as though I were a bit slow. "Sure, won't he have her address and telephone number upstairs?"

I smiled. "Upstairs?"

"Of course! I have all his stuff upstairs. His computer, all his papers, his diary . . . everything. I mean, until today . . ." Her face started to fold up into wet grief again. "We had no idea if he was coming back. He might have turned up at any time, walked through the door . . . !"

I watched her a moment, trying to conceive what kind of hell she must be going through. I couldn't even begin. I turned to Jim. I saw the same hell behind his eyes, but I knew from his face he was going to keep it together until we were gone, until Kathleen couldn't see him.

I said, "We need to take his things away and examine them. Have you any objection? It will all be returned to you after the investigation."

"We have no objection. Take what you need. Just catch the bastard who did this to our son."

I pulled out my phone and called the 43rd. "I need a CSI team to collect evidence from the following address . . ." I told her where it was. Then added, "It is just papers and IT stuff. No, no body."

When I hung up, Kathleen said, "Of course, it all depends how much was taken in the burglary."

Dehan sat back and sighed. I tried not to look at her. "Burglary?"

"Didn't it all happen at the same feckin' time. They say it never rains but it pours. The very night after he never came home, didn't we have a feckin' break-in? They went into his room, God alone knows what they expected to find up there . . ."

Jim shrugged. "The policeman said it was probably opportunistic, you know, broke in on the off chance."

I stared at them both for a moment, trying to fathom the depths of human stupidity.

"It didn't occur to you, or the cop, that his disappearance and the break-in might be connected?"

They looked blank. Kathleen said, "No. Why would it?"

I smiled. "Sure, why would it? Did anything go missing from Sean's room?"

"I couldn't tell you," said Jim. "He kept all his stuff very private. Nobody was allowed to touch it, but I wouldn't have thought so. Sure, they left the computer, didn't they? A real fancy one at that, and who'd be interested in a lot of papers? So you're probably all right."

I nodded and looked at Dehan. "No doubt." I made to stand. "We won't take up any more of your time. A van will be here shortly to bag up and take the stuff from Sean's room. Please don't go in there or disturb anything. We'll keep you posted as to any developments."

We left them holding each other at the door and climbed into the Jag. Dehan frowned at me. "You don't want to look through his stuff before we leave?"

I shook my head. "I'm more interested in what isn't on the computer. We'll go over everything at our leisure back at the station, but I think we'll find anything of interest has already been taken." I fired up the engine. "Where to now, Dehan?"

She smiled. "Sure, isn't it time you spoke to Father O'Neil?"

I nodded. "It sure is."

Scan the QR code below to purchase GARDEN OF THE DAMNED.
Or go to: righthouse.com/garden-of-the-damned

www.ingramcontent.com/pod-product-compliance
Lightning Source LLC
Chambersburg PA
CBHW032123170626
46808CB00006B/2085